GRADUAL CLEARING

WEATHER REPORTS FROM THE HEART

ESSAYS BY KAREN ANDERSON

Karen Anderson

Arbutus Press
Traverse City, Michigan

Gradual Clearing: Weather Reports from the Heart
ISBN 978-1-933926-58-2
Copyright © 2017 Karen Anderson

Cover painting oil on linen 40x50" WATERFALL and
illustrations Copyright © 2017 Joyce Koskenmaki
web site: www.joycekoskenmaki.com
email: joycek@chartermi.net.

Arbutus Press
Traverse City, Michigan
editor@arbutuspress.com
www.Arbutuspress.com
facebook.com/arbutuspress

Other books by Karen Anderson

Letters from Karen, 1978
A Common Journey, 1980

WHAT HAPPINESS TO WAKE, ALIVE AGAIN,
INTO THIS SAME GRAY WORLD OF WINTER RAIN

SHOHA

CONTENTS

Foreword...9
Preface...11

Section 1: Scattered Clouds

Section 2: Rain Changing to Snow

Section 3: Gradual Clearing

Section 4: Visibility Unlimited

FOREWORD

When I was a kid, somebody told me that what we think of as a dream is really more like a memory, and dreaming is your mind sorting through and unpacking those memories. This provides the best analogy I can think of for the poetic essays Karen Anderson has been sharing with public radio listeners for more than decade. Her craft is to consider simple and often subtle details of everyday life—a family heirloom, moldy olives in the fridge, lilacs in bloom, the memory of a neighbor jogging down the street—and slowly distill wisdom from these ordinary bits of life through a process of careful remembering that can take years.

Her life is populated with a cast of characters from the past: an old boyfriend, a great aunt, a landlord and even people unknown to her, their exchanges penned on antique postcards. Even if, as she says, they no longer belong in her address book, they seem to haunt her and show up in her sketches of the world.

Affection for people is a trait Karen shares with her late mother. One of my favorite essays in this collection tells how her parents came to Traverse City from southern Michigan in the middle of life looking to enjoy paradise, a common motivation for all kinds of people living here on the shores of Grand Traverse Bay. But her mom "looked out the window and missed her neighbors." That's a useful cautionary tale for a community of people tempted to overestimate the pleasures and satisfaction that a beautiful landscape and even nature herself can finally offer. How fitting that her mom gave us a daughter who is engaged with both; as keen to contemplate her husband setting up the rain fly on the tent as she is observant of turtles enjoying the spring sunshine.

Peter Payette
Executive Director
Interlochen Public Radio

PREFACE

If my father hadn't been a dentist, he would have been a meteorologist. Fascinated by the weather, he announced his daily forecast: partly sunny, patchy fog, scattered flurries. And I soon realized that these phrases could also describe my moods and feelings—blustery, overcast, light and variable.

Thus, I selected *Gradual Clearing* as a title for this collection because I've often stared skyward and yearned to see the clouds lift, the sun emerge, bringing light and warmth. It speaks to my own search for clarity and meaning in my life.

I know I am not alone. Writing these personal essays for over forty years has confirmed that what is true for me is also—in some way—true for readers and listeners. When they respond to my work, it's not about me. It's about them. Somehow, their experience connects with mine.

Because our internal weather is pretty much the same, the cold fronts and gale warnings. The search for fair skies. Everybody wants meaning and clarity, gradual or otherwise.

To weather a storm means "to come safely through." It is my hope for all of us.

SECTION 1

SCATTERED CLOUDS

ADDRESS BOOK

The truth is, I need a new address book. The one I'm using is full of people who aren't even in my life anymore. Chuck and Cathy, for example, are listed as a couple. "We'll stay in touch," we said when they divorced. Then I divorced and we went in different directions, into new marriages, new lives.

Next, I see Erich's name, my daughter's first true love who died of cancer before he finished college. I told him I would start a scholarship in his name and I did, with the help of others who loved him.

Susan was my hairdresser, killed in a car crash at age fifty. Every morning when I wash my hair, I remember her advice about shampoo. "You just need a small amount," she said, pointing at the palm of her hand, "about the size of a dime."

And, there's the man I used to be in love with. Too complicated to continue and too wonderful to let go—but we did.

I need a new address book but if I got one, Erich wouldn't be in it or Susan or all those people I've loved and lost. Coming upon them this way, almost by chance, it seems as if they're still here.

My Grandparents' House

When I can't sleep, I go back to my grandparents' house and open the front door. There was no vestibule so you walked right into the living room. The coat closet had a stained glass window in blue and gold and violet.

I know that place by heart and can still stand in each room and picture the furnishings: the Victorian couch, the console radio, the four-poster twin beds upstairs. As a child, I often stayed overnight and it was a refuge from the confusions of my own home—my mother's sadness, my father's rage. Before I went to sleep, Nanna sat on the edge of the bed in her long nightgown and we talked awhile. "Are you warm enough?" she'd ask.

Looking back, I realize my grandparents' house was modest in size but it seemed huge to me. Huge and calm and welcoming. In the living room, I sat beside Grandpa and listened to him read Long-fellow's poem, *The Song of Hiawatha*. I liked the way the words made music.

In the dining room, our family gathered for special meals, using the good dishes from the big mahogany breakfront. Nanna always told the grandchildren, "Don't eat any more than you want." Which meant you could take an extra biscuit and not finish it.

It meant you had permission to be yourself, something I didn't feel anywhere else. Permission to sit on the floor of the coat closet in the dark and feel safe—watching the light come through the colored glass.

GOING STEADY

When I was fifteen years old, I went to visit my cousin who lived about 200 miles away. She was older than I and going steady with someone named Steve. I yearned to go steady but hadn't found anyone to share my yearning.

"I'm going to fix you up with Herbie," my cousin said.

As it turned out, Herb was a pleasant fellow who kindled no yearnings but was somebody to see a movie with. And while we were there, I noticed his arm was around my shoulders. "Maybe he likes me," I thought.

"I think Herbie likes you," my cousin said the next day. Nobody ever asked Herb and I never saw him again. But that didn't stop me from announcing to my girlfriends when I got home that I was going steady. It was a lie, of course—not even a white lie.

But it seemed like a gift, this fantasy boyfriend from another town. My cousin didn't know and even Herb didn't know. This was just between me and my girlfriends, me and my insecure self.

A few months later, a guy in my math class asked me out. "I thought you were going with Herb," my girlfriends said.

"Not anymore," I said. "I knew it wouldn't last."

BEAVER TREE

On the bank of the Betsie River is a tree with an hour-glass shape where beaver teeth have gnawed almost through the trunk. For some reason, the beaver gave up on this tree and left it to die slowly, standing up.

I point out the tree to my husband as we paddle past. "If only the beaver had stuck with it a little longer," I say.

"Too bad," he says, and I don't know whether he means the tree or the beaver.

The image of that gnawed trunk stays in my mind as we continue down the river. I think of all the times I've given up on projects or people when, with just a little more effort, I might have broken through to some kind of solution.

It was like that with my mother, both of us wanting to be closer but not knowing how. She was a homemaker and wanted the same for me, but I wanted something else, to have a career, to see the world. She praised my ambition and gave me aprons for my birthday.

And I resisted her control by distancing myself, by letting irritations lengthen into silences. Looking back, I wish I'd tried harder to find common ground—at her kitchen table or mine.

"Do you think that beaver will come back and finish the job?" I ask my husband.

"Don't know," he said. "Don't think so."

CIRCLE OF LIGHT

I am walking in my neighborhood on a winter day and see a mother pulling a small child on a sled. As they cross the street, the sled bounces down a curb and suddenly I feel the jolt and it is my mittened hands gripping the wooden frame.

Looking up, I see my father holding the rope and snow filtering through street lights. We have come outside after dinner and everything is glistening and quiet. Pulling the sled across the street, my father stops in the middle of an empty intersection.

"Hold on tight," he says, and begins to turn round and round, spinning my sled out from him in a wide arc, round and round in the feathery snow, in the glittering dark.

When my father finally stops, I beg for one more spin. "Hold on then," he says, and hurls me into orbit at the end of a loop of clothes line. The earth tilts and I lift off into the sparkling air, into a circle of light.

It is a moment of joy so alive inside me that sixty years later, I need only see a mother pulling a child on a sled and my mittened hands hold on tight.

Bonnie's Cottage

Finally, Bonnie invites me to spend a week at her family cottage, the cottage she's been telling me about all during eighth grade. Every day we will go swimming, she says, and sit on the dock and wait for boys to pick us up in their speedboats.

Now we're here and Bonnie says the lake is too cold for swimming. And although we sit on the dock every day, no boys come by. As it turns out, the only invitation to ride in a speedboat comes from Bonnie's dad on the last night of my visit.

"There are lots of little coves in this lake," he says as we steer away from shore, "so you have to know where you're going or you can get lost." Bonnie's cottage quickly disappears from view and the sky deepens from violet to indigo.

The air is cold and the noise of the motor throbs in my ears. I can see nothing but black water all around us, tiny stars overhead. The boat keeps plunging into darkness and I feel terrified and enormously alive. As it turns out, nothing has turned out like I thought it would, and the best part of the visit is something I never thought of.

"You have to know where you're going," Bonnie's dad says. And he does.

DRAGONS UNDER THE BED

Even with the fan going, the temperature in the bedroom must be close to ninety. "Are you sure you want to sleep with that sheet on?" I ask my daughter.

"Yes," Sara says in her little-girl voice. I rarely hear that voice anymore now that she is an adult, and I enjoy this chance to tuck her into bed.

"That sheet makes you feel safe, doesn't it?" I say.

"It protects me from dragons under the bed," she says, laughing. We both laugh, remembering when we used to check for dragons every night.

"Have you checked?" I ask. "Maybe they're gone for good now."

"I don't think they're ever gone," she says. I thought about it, the strange comfort of a sheet. Although we knew—probably even as children—that no cotton sheet could ever protect us from a dragon, we nonetheless felt safer.

We still feel safer, even as adults who know there are no dragons. There are plenty of other things to be afraid of, and those fears always seem larger when the lights go out and shadows gather.

"Silly, isn't it." Sara says.

"I don't know," I say. "I don't think so."

FRED'S VOICE

I met Fred at a fraternity party, a big burly guy with a handsome face and deep voice. Deep and dramatic. I knew before he told me that he dreamed of being an actor.

On our first date we rode his motorcycle twenty miles from campus to an old cider mill. With a gallon of cider and a bag of greasy donuts, we tramped the fields while Fred stood on stumps and declaimed lines from Shakespeare.

Then we headed to the football game where Fred stood up in the stands and declared, "The play's the thing!" It was entertaining at first, but the end came when Fred recited his own poetry beneath my dormitory window.

Thirty years later, I'm sitting in my living room watching the television series of *Lonesome Dove* when I hear that familiar voice. "Fred!" I cry, and sure enough, there he is, playing the role of Big Zwey, a buffalo hunter who isn't very bright but saves a woman from his rough companions. A character who could have been played for laughs but makes me care about his sad fate.

After the show, I check the Internet and discover that Frederick Coffin had played in over 80 films and countless television shows. He died in 2003 of lung cancer so it was too late to tell him I recognized his voice.

Fred never became a star but that wasn't his goal. He was an actor, and a good one.

BLINK BONNY

On a small island in Lake Erie called Hickory Island my great grandfather built a cottage—roomy and rustic with a wide porch across the front. Being Scottish, he named it "Blink Bonny," but we just called it "Hickory."

My grandmother and her sister inherited the cottage and the whole family gathered there every summer. The front lawn sloped down to a gravely beach where only the children went swimming, warned to not swallow the water. Nobody used the word "pollution" back then.

At the edge of the horizon was the shadow of a foreign country. *Canada*, my grandparents said. We often saw big freighters on the lake, hauling iron ore and grain to the east coast and overseas. Whenever one appeared, we'd stop what we were doing to watch. For the longest time, the huge boat seemed to be barely moving— and then was gone.

At dinner, the family ate together at a long oak table: potato salad, corn-on-the-cob, strawberry shortcake. And I felt so happy in this larger circle, I wished I could live forever in the attic bedroom with my cousins, sharing a bed under the slanted ceilings of knotty pine.

Instead, my grandmother and her sister sold the cottage, saying it was too costly to keep up, and the adults agreed. Nobody asked me. I was twelve years old, unable to grasp this finality while playing dolls on the daybed or walking down the backyard path between the tiger lilies.

My summers at Hickory were like those freighters, which seemed to move so slowly and then were gone.

Secret of Popularity

My mother puts the kitchen timer on the piano and sets it for 15 minutes. I sit on the bench and open my practice book. First I do scales and then stupid little songs about snowflakes and raindrops and spring flowers.

When the buzzer goes off, I quit playing and bolt from the piano. "You could at least finish the song," my mother says in her disappointed voice.

"I hate practicing." I open the refrigerator.

"But playing the piano will make you popular," my mother adds. Lord knows I want to be popular. I want to be Cookie Jones because all the boys love her. I wonder if she plays the piano, but she never talks to me.

I ask my piano teacher if I can play the songs I hear on the radio. Miss Wurzburg tells me that I'm not ready. Miss Wurzburg has dyed red hair under her little felt hat and rouge on her wrinkled cheeks. She lives alone with four cats.

"If Miss Wurzburg was so popular, why didn't she get married?" I ask my mother.

There is a long silence and she says, "If you want to stop at the end of the year, you can."

And I do.

HOLDING MY CUFFS

Pulling on my jacket, I notice how I automatically hold the cuffs of my shirt so the sleeves don't scrunch up. I've been doing this forever and haven't a clue who taught me or when.

Suddenly I'm aware of so many things that someone taught me as part of growing up: tying my shoes, buttoning a button, zipping a zipper, holding a pencil. Each task required some patient adult willing to help an impatient child.

Willing to keep encouraging me to try and try again—those countless adults—most of whom I cannot recall and surely never thanked.

At the time, those tasks seemed like a path to independence. Now, I realize I have depended on others every step of the way—and still do. I've also figured out it's okay to depend, to need; because others need me, too.

On a recent afternoon, I helped my granddaughter understand why a poem didn't have to rhyme. Then she helped me set up a Facebook page. A patient child helping an impatient adult.

So, I pull on my jacket, holding my cuffs, and remember how connected we are, each to each.

Each to all.

SCATTERED CLOUDS

I sit at the kitchen table with my husband before dinner. We're drinking a beer and eating pretzels and talking about the day. And while we're talking, I look over his shoulder out the window where gray-bellied clouds are moving across a blue sky.

There is gold light behind the clouds and I think that everything life could ever mean is about to be revealed. Maybe it's the beer; maybe not.

Should I interrupt my husband's narrative to alert him to this revelation? I remain silent and try to gaze out the window while appearing attentive to the conversation. I realize that cloud formations thrill and alarm me because they change while I am watching them.

There will never be another cloud like this one, I think. Even as I'm having this thought, the cloud is transforming itself into another shape or moving away or dissolving into nothingness. All of life is like this, of course—but it's not so visible, so obvious, so terrifying.

"What are you looking at?" my husband asks.

"Oh, just some clouds," I say, "They looked pretty with the light behind them. They're gone now."

ALL ABOUT LOVE

A friend sends me a CD of favorite songs and I slide the disc into my car stereo. Now, instead of the news, I'm listening to Frank Sinatra.

Instead of driving to the grocery store, I'm lying in my dormitory bed at college, singing "In the Wee Small Hours of the Morning." I know all the words and feelings by heart—by broken heart. I am nineteen years old again and have left my boyfriend back at home. He hasn't written for a week and I'm sure the relationship is over. Sure my life is over.

Frank Sinatra understands. He's there on the album cover in the light of a street lamp, smoking a cigarette and staring into the darkness. He knows what I know: love is everything and love is pain. I lift up the needle on my stereo and set it down again at the beginning of "Wee Small Hours."

Now, years later, I am pushing the replay button but I'm smiling instead of crying. Smiling to think how young I was, how pure my suffering, because it was almost untouched by experience. Now, I know how complicated love is, how it can be lost and found more than once.

Even so, I still sing along with Sinatra, sometimes in the wee small hours.

THREE CHINA DUCKS

Three china ducks sit on my desk. They're supposed to be mallards but the markings aren't very accurate. And besides, they're chipped and worn.

You might wonder why I keep them and I wonder that myself. I'm not one for knick-knacks, but when I glance at them, it isn't the ducks I see but my mother's beautiful hands—picking up each one and arranging them like a little family.

I can see the end table where those ducks lived, next to the orange chair. They shared space with a brass lamp and a round glass ash tray. One of my chores as a child was dusting the living room, and my mother showed me how to be careful with her many decorative pieces.

She had strong hands that moved with so much grace and assurance. My hands—like my body—seemed thin and awkward alongside her loveliness. I don't know how the mallards lost their toes and hope it wasn't my fault.

After my mother died, my father remarried and most of her things disappeared. Somehow the ugly ducks came to me. In recent years, I've been trying to get rid of stuff, and I've picked up the ducks more than once as I pack a box for Goodwill.

Then I put them down again. Not yet.

FORECAST

While the rest of the family is still getting dressed, my father has already walked around the motel parking lot for exercise. Popping back in the door, he says, "Rise and shine; the weather's fine."

We already know the weather isn't fine because we heard the thunder last night, and rain is pattering on the pavement. "It's clearing in the east," Dad says.

The sky looks gray in every direction as I climb in the car, and the only sunny side I believe in is the eggs I'm going to order for breakfast. It's raining harder when we leave the restaurant but my father is undaunted. "Clearing in the west," he says.

"You said east," I say. Dad laughs and holds the umbrella for us. "Sunny by noon," he says, and in spite of myself, I feel better.

Something magic happens to my dad on vacation. Suddenly he is making jokes and admiring the view and spending money without worrying. And what I wish for—even more than better weather— is that this cheerful person would come home with us. He doesn't resemble the stern, distant person who is my father the rest of the time.

I don't know which way is east, but there's a bright line along the horizon. "By noon," he says. "You'll see."

SCHOOL BUS DRIVER

When my daughter was in elementary school, we lived on a hill in the woods. The school bus picked her up at the bottom of the hill and in the afternoon I would watch for her to come home.

In the winter, the first thing I saw was the top of her stocking cap bobbing up the path between the trees. Seeing that bright red hat against the white landscape always made me smile—and murmur a silent thank you to the school bus driver.

Once, when she was late, I was convinced her bus had toppled into a ditch and I was in tears by the time she arrived.

"I just stopped to play," she said. "Don't worry, Mom." But there were so many hills and so much snow.

I was in awe of bus drivers, navigating those big awkward machines up and down those narrow slippery roads. Not to mention the noise factor behind them in the seats.

In their capable hands they held not only a huge steering wheel but the well-being of every parent on their route. So I have to believe there's a special corner of heaven reserved for these saints where the pavement is always dry.

OLIVES

My mother's refrigerator was jam-packed—with jam and every other foodstuff that could be crammed onto its shelves. "Please find me some black olives," she'd say, and I would dive into the chaos.

"We have three jars of black olives," I would finally announce. "Two are moldy."

"Oh, goodness!" she'd say as if surprised, though she had bought the jars herself. "Throw them away before your father gets home."

Inheriting my father's frugality, I keep a Spartan refrigerator. At any given moment, I know exactly what's in it and, if I can't see the back wall, I get anxious. My daughter has had the opposite reaction. "I always feel hungry when I look in our refrigerator," she used to say. I tried to explain about the moldy olives.

Now she's an adult and keeps a refrigerator that looks just like my mother's. Opening the produce drawer, I see the same head of lettuce I saw the last time I was there—weeks ago. I take it out, then put it back.

The Bible says that the sins of the fathers are visited upon their children and their children's children. Mothers, too, evidently. Lord knows I've tried to manage the mayhem. But there it is, behind the casserole leftovers, another jar of olives.

Neutrogena

It's likely that Neutrogena soap is still good for my skin, but I use it because of the smell, slightly medicinal and piney. More than anything else, that familiar scent evokes my college years.

Leaning over one of the sinks in my dormitory bathroom, I would suds up my face, moving my fingers around in little circles like my mother taught me, rinsing thoroughly and patting the skin dry. Then, in the unforgiving fluorescent light, I would examine my complexion for blemishes.

I loved the tight, fresh feel of my skin after I washed my face. That feeling, along with the distinctive smell of Neutrogena, came to signal a sense of hopefulness and discovery. About the date that was picking me up that night, about the life that lay ahead.

College was a source of continuous learning, in the classroom and beyond. I was studying with professors who were passionate about Shakespeare or Chaucer or Scott Fitzgerald—and invited me to find my own passions. One of them turned out to be Emily Dickinson. Another was a fraternity boy named Denny.

Everything seemed possible in those days and at the end of the day, I would lean over the sink again and wash my face before bed.

LENTEN BREAKFAST

I get up earlier than usual on a school morning and my father is already shaving in the bathroom. "Well, well," he says, "Looks like my date is ready."

"Aw, Dad, I'm still in my pajamas!" But my outfit is laid out on the bed, my red plaid dress and patent leather shoes. Today is the Father-Daughter Lenten Breakfast at our church.

The long tables are set with white cloths and a purple ribbon down the middle. Bouquets of daffodils alternate with baskets of hot cross buns. "Where do you want to sit?" my father asks and I let him choose. He looks handsome in his dark suit.

Before we eat, the minister leads everyone in a prayer. Then he invites the fathers to introduce their daughters. I have to stand up, and my heart is beating so loudly I can hardly hear my father but I think he uses the word proud.

This breakfast is the only thing my father and I do together except dishes and homework. "You're not eating very much," he says. "You feel okay?"

I nod vigorously and take a bite of eggs. I know that Lent is supposed to be time when you give up something, so it seems strange that I get something I want more than anything. "I'm having a great time," I say.

CRICK

Sometimes when I visited my grandmother, she would take me with her to Dr. Dursom's house. He was a retired chiropractor, she explained, who still gave what she called "adjustments" to friends of the family for one dollar.

I didn't know what an adjustment was and Dr. Dursom scared me a little—a big man with a tall brush cut who smoked cigars. While my grandmother went upstairs with the doctor, I sat in the parlor with Mrs. Dursom, a kindly woman with tight gray curls, who offered me lemonade.

The whole thing seemed a little strange to me. Dr. Dursom wasn't anything like the white-coated doctors I was used to but since my grandmother was a sensible woman who never got sick, I figured she must know what she was doing.

Then one morning I woke up with a terrible crick in my neck. My mother and grandmother agreed at once and soon I was following Dr. Dursom upstairs. He sat me on a stool and gave my neck a quick twist. The crick was gone!

And for the first time, I understood that healing could happen in many different places. Even an old bedroom that smelled like cigars.

Worth a dollar, for sure. Worth more than that.

BETTER THAN

No one used the term "sex education" when I was growing up; in fact, no one used the word "sex." Whatever information we gathered about this mystery was from glimpses and whispers, from eavesdropping on adults and gossiping with peers.

In junior high school, I had a group of girlfriends that included a skinny blond named Barb. We often gathered at her house because she had an older brother who kept copies of *Playboy Magazine* in his closet.

When he was gone, we snuck into his bedroom to peek at those forbidden pages, comparing ourselves unfavorably with the bunnies. But while *Playboy* was a fantasy, we found a reality closer to home.

Barb's parents seemed to really enjoy each other's company and had managed to keep the romance going that we only saw in movies. One night, we overheard the two of them talking.

"I'm going to take a hot bath," Barb's mom said. "Soaking in the tub is the most wonderful feeling."

"Better than?" her dad asked.

"Not as good as," she answered.

Those became our watchwords: "Not as good as." They promised more than *Playboy*, more than Hollywood. Because they left everything to the imagination.

SCHNITZELBANK

When I was growing up in Grand Rapids, my family sometimes went to dinner at a German restaurant called the "Schnitzelbank." Before the meal, my parents enjoyed having a cocktail—a Manhattan for my father, Whiskey Sour for my mother—while my brother Bob and I finished off the basket of bread.

It was good dark German rye with whole seeds and hard crusts, unlike anything we ate at home. When the waitress finally came, our father would say, "Order whatever you want," and we did, forgetting we were already full.

Although Bob and I could never clean our plates, Dad never scolded. At home he pinched every penny, but when we went out for dinner he didn't count the cost. "I wish they didn't put prices on menus," he said.

Looking back, I'm pretty sure my parents would have enjoyed the Schnitzelbank more without two fidgety children at the table. But they wanted us to learn how to read a menu and order a meal and calculate the right tip. We even learned not to eat all the bread in the basket.

Nowadays, Bob and I enjoy having a cocktail before dinner, too, and we recently shared a toast at a favorite pub. "To the parents," he said, "and the Schnitzelbank."

"Order whatever you want," I said.

Down to Basics

After a day of hiking and canoeing, my husband and I sit by the campfire until fatigue persuades me to crawl into our tent. Zipping up my sleeping bag, I review what's important.

It's not the same checklist I have at home when I often fall asleep reviewing what work assignments await me the following day, or what's in the refrigerator for supper. No, my sleeping bag list is much more basic and carefully prioritized.

Am I well? Am I safe? Warm? Dry? Fed? Because if I'm not well, I won't even care whether I'm safe and if I'm not safe, I won't care whether I'm warm and dry. And even food comes after health and safety.

And if I am well, safe, warm, dry, fed, I am deeply grateful. Alongside these basics, I'm not very concerned about whether I'm loved, recognized, or fulfilling my purpose in life. It's a good reminder, this process, that if basic needs aren't met, nothing else matters very much.

A reminder that many in our community and the world do not have basic needs met. And when I'm tempted to judge or assume or prescribe—I'm probably wrong. And probably not doing enough to change it.

ELM

Every time I travel a certain highway south of Traverse City, I look for a single elm tree on the north side of the road. A glorious, healthy elm that stands out against the oaks and maples because of its graceful vase-like form and immense height.

Somehow, it survived the blight of Dutch elm disease that wiped its cousins off the map over fifty years ago in Michigan. Driving by that rare tree, I am filled with gratitude and respect.

My grandmother had two elms in her front yard in Grand Rapids which she watered as tenderly as her garden in the back. When my grandfather died and she was alone, those trees became even more valuable as companions and guardians. If they could survive in all weathers, so could she.

Then the City came and cut them down in an effort to control Dutch elm disease. Suddenly there were two holes in the sky and my grandmother never recovered from this loss. None of us did.

Oaks and maples are wonderful, of course, and pines are a special feature of our northern region. But each time I see that surviving elm on the highway south of town, I recall that nothing has replaced them—their lovely shape and stature.

They used to be everywhere.

41

MISS CURRY

Miss Curry was my eleventh grade English teacher, a small woman with thick glasses and fuzzy brown hair. After class one day, she invited me to join a creative writing group and I accepted, although I had no sense of myself as a writer.

There were six of us that evening—six awkward students who didn't fit in at school but who were welcome in Miss Curry's living room where we sat in a circle and read our secret poems and stories.

Mostly I stared at Miss Curry's elegant apartment with its high ceilings and walls of books. We discovered she had studied in Paris and knew all kinds of famous artists and writers. And it occurred to me that this woman had a rich and meaningful life that didn't look anything like my mother's.

Later, we joined Miss Curry in her cluttered kitchen to make spaghetti, laughing together like old friends. It was the friendship that kept us coming back month after month, along with Miss Curry's stubborn belief in our potential.

We never stopped coming back, introducing her to our spouses and our children. Her name was Nelle but I always called her Miss Curry. She was my teacher, as long as she lived—and longer.

DON'T CONTRADICT

Freedom of speech, while guaranteed in the Constitution, was not encouraged in my home when I was growing up. I could speak my mind only if I agreed with my parents. Otherwise, I was told, "Don't contradict."

When they offered me an allowance of a dime a week, I objected. Objection overruled. When I claimed that an early curfew cramped my style, they said, "Exactly."

When Kennedy ran for president, I was too young to vote but spoke in his favor. My father was scornful. "The country will never elect a Catholic," he said. This time I didn't have to contradict; the voters did it for me.

Finally, as a young adult, I explored the issues for myself and made up my own mind. And I've concluded that this is every child's responsibility. I said this to a friend who responded, "And the parents should encourage it."

It's possible, of course, that grown-up children will choose to believe what they were taught, but it must be a well-researched choice. As it turned out, I was pretty big on curfews myself when my daughter was young.

She contradicted but I expected that. Tried to *encourage* it. Tried to listen, to not say, "Because I said so." Hard work, this growing up. For children and for parents.

SCARS

I have a scar on my face, under my right cheek bone. Not very large, maybe an inch long. I never notice it because I've never seen my face without it.

I was five years old when I pulled my little wagon several blocks from my house to ride down a long, steep hill. Just as I pushed off, my friend Tommy jumped on behind me, and we ran off the sidewalk into a rusty barbwire fence.

Something sharp poked my face and I screamed. Tommy ran away and I held the skirt of my dress up against my cheek. By the time I walked home, the green and white plaid was soaked with red. My mother cried and called my father to ask if she should take me to the hospital. "A band aid will probably do the job," he said.

The scar was not disfiguring, but my mother apologized the rest of my life for not having taken me to get stitches. "It's okay, Mom," I said. "It's who I am."

Scars don't go away. That's why they're called scars. Some are physical, others emotional. Visible or invisible. Regardless, we collect a lot of them in a lifetime—evidence that we've been hurt. Also that we've healed.

LUNCH WITH GRANDPA

When my grandfather invited me to go out to lunch, it wasn't anyplace fancy, just the Booth Dairy a few blocks away. Booth's was mostly a place to buy milk and ice cream, but they also had a little lunch counter where you could order sandwiches.

I ordered peanut butter and jelly and Grandpa ordered ham on rye. While we waited for our food, Grandpa drank coffee and I spun myself around on the chrome stool. If I pushed off with my feet, I could go really fast.

"Grandpa, you should try this!" I exclaimed.

"It looks like fun," he said, but he didn't try it. The man behind the counter brought me a glass of white milk with chocolate syrup in the bottom and a long spoon.

"Thought you might like to stir this up yourself," he said. The sandwiches came on paper plates with potato chips. Grandpa got a pickle with his. The peanut butter and jelly tasted funny, not nearly as good as the ones I ate at home.

"How's your lunch, Scout?" Grandpa asked.

"I really like the stir-up milk."

Booth's Dairy wasn't a fancy place, and the sandwiches weren't very good. I don't know whether my Grampa took me there a hundred times or only once, but I've remembered it forever, sitting at the counter together.

Merganser Math

On a morning in late spring, my husband and I canoe a section of the Manistee River. Close to shore a merganser duck is swimming with ten ducklings in a row behind her. *Ten.*

So I start to wonder, "Can mergansers count?" How would she know if one of her babies was missing if she can't count? Yet, as we glide past her, Mother Merganser doesn't even turn her handsome brown head to check on her brood. She trusts that they are right there—all ten of them. And they are, in one long undulating line.

I realize I'm asking the wrong question. What I want to know is whether the merganser can take care of her babies and clearly, the answer is yes.

For all I know, she might be wondering why I need a big aluminum tub and a wooden stick to navigate this river. Why can't I just slide into the water and paddle with my feet?

After all, a human being is only one way of being. My worldview is so narrow, and the world is so wide. Wide and mysterious and utterly beyond my reckoning, even with numbers.

OLDEN DAYS

"Tell me what life was like in the olden days," I used to say to my dad. By this I meant when he was a kid like me. He told me that his family had an ice box instead of a refrigerator.

"The ice melted, of course," my father said, "so I rigged up a little tube to drain the water out into the back yard. My mother was so pleased." I thought about our huge refrigerator which hummed quietly day and night, never needing attention, and was glad I didn't live in the olden days. I decided I would always live right here in the present.

I was one of the grandchildren and we were surrounded by parents and grandparents. Then slowly, as slowly as ice melting, our grandparents died and then our parents died, too. While my cousins, my brother and I were still calling ourselves "the grandchildren," we were becoming the grandparents.

"When I was a kid, a horse and wagon delivered the milk to my neighborhood." I hear the voice telling this story and am surprised to find it's mine. How did my childhood become the olden days?

"A horse and wagon?" my granddaughter asks.

"Yes," I say, "and the horse knew which houses to stop at all along the street."

SECTION 2

RAIN CHANGING TO SNOW

AWAKE AT NIGHT

My mother told me that when she was a little girl, there were times she couldn't sleep at night. "I would lie in bed and imagine that somewhere in the world a single gas station was open," she said. "Then I didn't feel so lonely and could go back to sleep."

Her story comforted me, too, when I was awake in the quiet darkness. I could picture that same gas station—the pump out front and a light on inside, with one guy at a desk reading a magazine. Somehow, the world wasn't so scary and I wasn't so alone.

Of course, even when my mother was a child, there must have been a hospital open at night or a police station. And after all, it was daytime on the other side of the planet. But those things don't necessarily occur to a small child. They didn't occur to me.

Just recently, I was remembering my mother's imaginary gas station when I couldn't sleep—and thought that today, there are countless businesses open twenty-four hours. And I wondered, why am I not comforted?

Because everything feels too wide-awake now, too round-the-clock, nonstop. Hectic, demanding, exhausting. I can't find the OFF button—for the world, or for my mind. So, I picture that single gas station, a light on inside.

BAD MOTHER

"Mom, can I have this?" my daughter asked. We were browsing in a toy store and Sara had picked up one of those little wooden animals with jointed legs that move when you push on the base.

"No," I said. "You'd be bored with that in ten minutes."

Like a good daughter, Sara put it back on the shelf. Like a bad mother, I put it out of my mind. Years later she remembered this experience.

"I was just crushed," she said.

"I really said that?" I asked.

"You really said that."

I had a vision of myself as a small child, laboring for hours to make a doll out of corn silk. The adults praised my efforts. Nobody said, "That corn silk will be all dried up by morning." I found that out for myself.

Of course I apologized to Sara—long after the fact—and bought her a little wooden donkey with jointed legs. Since then, we have exchanged a score of wooden lions and horses and cats and cows. "You'll be bored with this in ten minutes," we tell each other and laugh. But I wince, too.

"I really said that?" I ask again.

"You really did."

CATALPA

The tree was already huge when we bought the house many years ago, a handsome catalpa that stood beside the back door with an eye bolt sticking out where previous owners might have hooked one end of a hammock.

Two enormous limbs reached high above our house and the neighbor's house, and its broad leaves provided blessed shade. As the seasons passed, the eye bolt disappeared into the trunk and then bark started falling off.

"But it leaves out beautifully," I said to the forester who came to look.

"Its vascular system is healthy," he said, "but structurally, it's failing." He pointed out where lightning had struck one of the main branches long ago. "There's rot inside, and that big canopy is very heavy."

Hearing this verdict, I couldn't speak. "If the tree was standing in a field," he said, "we could let it live out its normal life." Now our neighbor's house was at risk, our house too. But oh, this living tree that had hurt no one, that was my friend.

A crew came to take it down at the end of May. The chain saws screamed all day and finally the enormous trunk lay on its side, ten feet around, a hundred rings. Our back yard was a tangle of branches and every one held tiny green leaves.

I left the house to escape the noise and ran into a friend. She asked how I was doing. "Not so well," I said. "We had to take our catalpa tree down today."

"And you loved it," she said. I stood there crying.

Someone's Papers

I open the front door to pick up the newspaper and notice trash on the grass next to the curb. "What is this?" I think irritably as I go out to pick it up. But it's not trash. It is somebody's personal papers, folded up and soaking wet from last night's rain.

I carefully unfold them on the kitchen counter and discover a birth certificate, legal papers, credit cards, business cards, and a pile of receipts and notes—belonging to a young man.

And as I look through these papers, I feel vaguely uncomfortable, as if I am invading his privacy. But I am searching for a phone number so I can let him know his papers are safe and will be returned. I find an address but no phone number and he's not in the phone book.

I think of all the things I've lost over the years and how few have been recovered. A watch, a wallet, a precious ring, an intimate journal. The sting of these losses never quite eases. How could I have been so careless, so stupid?

I lay the young man's soggy documents on paper towels to dry. And all day long, it's as if there is a stranger in the house, someone I should include in the conversation.

The next day, I find a sturdy envelope, fold up the personal papers, and put them in the mail.

BLIZZARD CONDITIONS

On the radio, the weatherman announces, "Blizzard conditions." I stare out the window at blowing snow, poor visibility. And I have to admit, it's just *beautiful*!

Easy for me to say because I'm standing here in my nice warm kitchen. The storm is wild and wonderful as long as I don't have to travel. As long as my loved ones don't have to travel. I review the list, and am grateful they're all at home today or living far south where no blizzards threaten.

But beyond my circle are many others who do have to travel— friends and acquaintances and strangers. Many who must venture out onto those treacherous roads, peering through white-outs and straining to see the yellow line.

I've traveled many miles in blizzard conditions myself and know the terror, the exhaustion. When the windshield wipers can't keep up, when the brakes don't grab, when the road disappears from view.

Probably there's never a time when someone isn't traveling through bad weather, when someone isn't at risk. We live in a world where loveliness and danger exist side-by-side.

Can I still celebrate the beauty? I think I must. Spruce boughs release great clouds of snow into the wind.

PRETZELS

Everywhere I look, something needs fixing, cleaning, organizing. Weeds in the garden, dust balls under the table, papers on my desk. I start in the kitchen, down on my knees with a bucket and sponge, finding cat toys and dried-up broccoli and pretzels. Lots of pretzels as I scrub.

But finally, the old hardwood floor shines, really shines. By suppertime, I can already see a footprint in the doorway. Mine! I bang the bucket around on my way to the basement and go pull weeds.

No matter how hard I try, imperfections win, hands down. Dirty hands. So here's my question: is there a way to celebrate the mess as proof of being alive in this complex, crazy world? As proof that I belong here, that everybody belongs, come as we are, imperfect?

It is a kind of solace to know we're all struggling to make sense of, to make peace with, make a difference in the midst of so much that is ugly, hurtful, wrong. And we keep muddling through, recycling cans and bottles and grief. We even apologize, sometimes, for the pain *we've* caused.

So I'm here again, on my knees with a sponge trying to make some minor improvements and grateful for the privilege. The *responsibility*.

DEATH OF A NEIGHBOR

I am scanning the obituaries in the local paper when I see the name of a neighbor, someone who lived not far from me. I didn't know she was ill, and I feel strangely empty and sad.

We weren't friends, really, but I knew her name and a little about her work and family. This is a small town, and if you live here long enough, you run into a lot of people. She and I said hello occasionally at the grocery store or library.

But while I gaze at her picture and read her obituary, I recall that I didn't like her. Which meant I would acknowledge her when we met but didn't stop to talk. Didn't make an effort to get better acquainted.

And when I try to remember why I didn't like her, I cannot think of a single reason. Whatever triggered my irritation was so insignificant, it has vanished. While the irritation remained. Now my sorrow about her death expands to include my own smallness, my petty grievances. I am ashamed to admit how these unexamined opinions linger—and limit my life.

Sometimes it's too late to make amends. I close the newspaper and sip my cold coffee. She was my neighbor and I never thought much about her until now. I can remember her jogging slowly down the street, her face flushed. A pretty woman.

LOSING TOUCH

I'm having lunch with a friend and ask her about a man we both know. "What do you hear from Jay?"

She answers matter-of-factly. "Oh, he died of a heart attack a few years ago."

Died? That can't be possible. True, he and I had not been in contact recently, but I always assumed we'd reconnect somehow.

Jay was a Christian minister and I am a Unitarian, and we used our differences to explore the big questions in some of the most nourishing conversations I've ever had. What was the purpose of religion, we asked.

"To support each other in our quest for the abundant life," Jay said, and further alarmed his congregation by announcing, "Life is an open question. Meanings aren't out there waiting to be discovered; we move into the world and create meanings."

When he transferred to a more liberal church in another state, we lost touch. "Lost touch." The phrase sounds so casual, as if it happened by accident. But we let it happen. In books and movies, all the loose ends get tied up. Foolishly, I thought life would be the same.

Now, it seems as if life is unraveling as I go and that this might be the larger reality, the deeper truth. "When everything is said and done," we say, as if that were possible. It's not. So, while there's time, I must say and do the things that matter. Must stay in touch.

To Last

The shoe repairman glances up as I walk into his tiny shop.

"I'm having my kitchen remodeled," I say, "and when the guys pulled the cabinets off the walls, they found this in the rafters." I haul a leather boot out of my backpack. "I'm hoping you can tell me something about it."

"It's old," he says with a half-smile. "Fifty years, at least. Star brand or Wolverine." He turns the boot upside down where it has been re-soled and re-heeled, rather crudely.

"Did those repairs himself," the man says. "Everybody had their own last." I don't know what he means. "L-A-S-T," he says and points to the metal form of an upside-down shoe anchored to his bench.

"But don't you wonder how the boot got into the rafters?" I ask. The repairman isn't interested in that part of the story. He is showing me some old lasts on a shelf, attached to stumps.

"Used them to last a shoe," he says, turning the word into a verb.

I think about how people used to try hard to last things. Today, almost everything is disposable. And I leave his shop wishing we could last more of what we have—boots, clothes, computers, friendships, marriages. All of it.

SPECIAL OFFER

The picture on the back of my comic book looked so real. World War II army soldiers were firing guns and running with bayonets. Best of all, you could get a hundred for just one dollar!

I didn't want them for myself but for my younger brother. Bob had a few toy soldiers but he didn't have a hundred! I didn't have a dollar either but I saved my allowance and finally mailed in the coupon. When the package arrived, it looked pretty small for a hundred soldiers, and then I found out why.

The soldiers were tiny, two-dimensional cutouts in thin gray plastic. They didn't even stand up. "Oh, Mom," I cried, "They're not like the picture!"

"No, they're not," she said, "but it was nice of you to do that for Bob."

I didn't feel nice. I felt stupid and angry for believing in that Special Offer, for believing you could get a hundred soldiers for a dollar.

It was too good to be true, of course, and now I knew what that meant. A hard lesson and costly, but I've always remembered it. Also remembered how Bob thanked me.

Brown Sweater

Glancing down, I see a bug on my sweater—but no, it's just one of a million little balls of wool that have pilled up on this ancient garment. And as I look more closely, I am suddenly and properly embarrassed.

How can I wear this ugly old thing? The cuffs are crusty with food, the sleeves fuzzy with cat hair, and the pockets stuffed with Kleenex. It is the most disgusting sweater on the planet, hands down, and I put it on every day.

I don't have to tell you why. It's comfortable, that's why. Warm and cozy and familiar. And, of course, mostly invisible to me who lives on the inside.

Why has no one in my household asked me to abandon this grotesque relic? Probably because other members of my family have similar items in their wardrobes. None quite this bad, perhaps, but close.

You'll have to take my word for it that this L.L. Bean "field sweater" was once rather handsome—a rich brown zip-up cardigan with a snug collar and patches on the elbows—a gift to myself when it was featured on the cover of the catalog.

But I never bought it to make a fashion statement, only to keep me warm. To welcome me with open arms and grungy cuffs, a little the worse for wear. Also better.

God's Begonia

I never expected to be doing missionary work, hampered as I am by doubt in the existence of God. It began when our book group met at a church and I discovered a gorgeous huge begonia in the hallway. Plucking off two shiny leaves, I stashed them in my purse.

They refused to root in water (protesting my theft) so I stuck them a pot of dirt. Then my daughter was diagnosed with cancer just as she became engaged to be married. "What kind of God would do this?" I raged. Not any kind I could believe in.

So, I put my faith in modern medicine and human love—and we kept planning the wedding. In the morning, I took Sara to treatments, in the afternoon to dress fittings. And meanwhile, on my windowsill, a tender green leaf pushed up alongside the stolen ones. I wept to see it.

"It could be a coincidence," I thought, "or it could be a sign." Slowly, slowly, Sara was getting well. That was many years ago now and she is fine, married to the same good man and working happily as a librarian.

People sometimes ask about the enormous plant in my living room. "It's God's Begonia," I tell them, "and it's taken over my life." From its leaves I have started dozens of other plants, which I give away to anyone who needs a gift of healing.

Recipients tell me that they, too, give away plants. So the missionary work continues, taking root in different pots, different windows.

LEAVES FOR MILDRED

Mildred was a large, middle-aged woman who sat in the back row of my workshop and told me she had to leave at the break. "My husband is in the hospital," she said, and I wondered if she was just bored.

A few weeks later, I received a letter from Mildred, a letter postmarked Hawaii. "My husband died that afternoon," she wrote, "and I sold my house and moved to Honolulu to be near my daughter."

Mildred and I corresponded for over twenty years although I never saw her again. We were both inclined to romance and melancholy—and she missed the seasons terribly, especially the aching loveliness of autumn. So it was that my daughter and I began to collect leaves each fall and send them to Mildred.

"My grandchildren take them to school for show-and-tell," she wrote, "and then we make a small bonfire on my balcony so we can smell the smoke."

Mildred died many years ago but I still miss her. Recently, while staring at the red and orange and yellow leaves on the sidewalk, I wondered where she was. And then I knew that she was right there, shining up at me in all the bright colors.

FALLING OUT OF LOVE

It was a bad time to fall out of love. For one thing, my husband and I were on vacation. For another, we were trapped in one small room of a bed and breakfast in Mallaig, Scotland, a room already crowded with furniture and figurines.

Mallaig was a fishing village across from the Isle of Skye, where we were headed the following day. "Isle of Skye" had sounded like a romantic destination until I found out that "skye" didn't mean a vast expanse of blue overhead but was a Gaelic word for "mist."

"How fitting," I thought bitterly, feeling tired of trying to see my way clear. To *make* myself clear. The argument was a familiar one, about calling ahead for reservations. I wanted to call and know; Dick wanted to wait and see.

Sitting in a local pub, we drained our pints of dark Scottish ale and declared the relationship hopeless. I wondered if I had the energy to start over with someone new. Start over without any history. As if that were possible.

We ate breakfast in a sunny dining room overlooking the harbor. "It's not about reservations," I said finally. "It's about feeling safe." Growing up in a chaotic home—too much anger and alcohol—I sometimes wanted a comfort zone more than an adventure. To take refuge instead of taking risks.

Dick nodded. He knew. We'd been over this ground before, although the place names were different. We held hands on the ferry and watched the island come toward us out of the mist.

PARADISE

In 1964, when they were middle-aged, my parents moved to Traverse City, Michigan, from Grand Rapids, where they had lived all their lives. The reason for the move was a job offer my father had received from the State Hospital.

He had been a dentist in private practice but was unable to save enough for retirement. As a dentist at the State Hospital, he could earn a pension. Besides, "Traverse City is paradise," he said. "Haven't we vacationed there for years?"

"Yes," my mother said, "but we have never lived there." Yet, as a career homemaker with no income of her own, she had no choice but to go.

They bought an old farmhouse outside of town with a view of the bay. "If we're going to live in Traverse City, we might as well see the water," my father said. My mother looked out the window and missed her neighbors. There was no one next door or across the street, no one to have coffee with, share recipes—to greet, to call, to count on.

My mother eventually got acquainted in Traverse City but new friends weren't like old friends. She died the year after my father retired. "It's hard to start over at this age," she said once.

Even in paradise.

RUNOFF

My husband and I are canoeing the Manistee River in early spring. This might be our favorite season because the water is high and fast—and there are no black flies yet. We can still see through the woods and catch a glimpse of deer, beaver, turkeys.

The hard work belongs to Dick, who sits in the stern and guides us around fallen trees and through tumbling rapids. Up in the bow, I only have to keep paddling and keep watch.

This time of year, the water is muddy with runoff from melting snow. My life feels the same, clogged with debris from the past, cloudy with regrets. All the answers I thought I had found seem obscure now and lost from view.

But the river keeps going, pushing against its banks with relentless movement. Whatever it is asked to carry, however far, it shoulders with fierce energy. Including me and my various confusions. Inviting me to lighten up and let go. Let the silt and sadness sink out of sight. The river knows what it means to move on, knows there isn't any choice.

A red leaf from last fall twirls in the current and vanishes around a bend. And on a cold bright morning, I am strangely healed.

TURQUOISE SILK DRESS

I am looking through my button box and pick up a small cloth-covered button. "Turquoise silk," I murmur, remembering the dress it came from, a dress I wore only once.

It was elegant and expensive and I bought it to attend a dance with a law student. I was a senior in college and liked being able to say I was dating a law student. The fellow himself was actually rather dull.

Still, I bought the turquoise silk dress because I wanted to dazzle him or his friends or myself. Sometimes it is enough to feel dazzling, even if you're the only one who knows. Before the dance, a group of couples went to a fine restaurant for dinner.

I ordered broiled lamb chops and they arrived on a sizzling metal platter, splattering grease all over the front of my turquoise dress. Looking down at the dark spots on the bright silk, I felt sick to my stomach. The waiter brought baking soda to soak up the grease, and I sat there with white splotches across my chest while others laughed and ate their meals.

I don't know why I saved a button from that ruined turquoise dress. Maybe because I loved it so much—or because I loved the girl who felt dazzling for an hour.

BEING LOVED

My first year in college I met a fellow who was a couple years older. A good-looking, take-charge kind of guy who made me feel special and cherished. Soon, he persuaded me to go steady and then he began talking marriage.

I was dazzled by his attention, so dazzled that I couldn't see clearly, couldn't see him at all—his interests and goals—and whether we were really compatible. But I convinced myself that I loved him, only to realize much later that I had been in love with *being* loved.

That was long ago and now I have two young granddaughters who are very interested in love, especially the romantic kind. I told them about my college boyfriend, how flattered I was and how foolish.

"What did you do?" they asked.

"I finally ended it," I said. "Much later than I should have. And I regret how I hurt him."

One of these granddaughters announced a few months later that she had broken up with a boy she'd been dating. "I remembered your story," she said, "about being in love with being loved."

We nodded together, sipping our cherry-mint tea. "It's pretty seductive," I said and we laughed a little. Cried a little.

Home Home

The picture side of the postcard shows a horse and buggy in the middle of a residential street with small maple trees in front of each house. Today, those same maples tower over Eighth Street in Traverse City, Michigan, not far from where I live.

The postcard was mailed a hundred years ago on March 13, 1917 to a "Miss M. Edgecomb" in Grand Rapids, the message brief:

> *Dear Daughter, I waited for you last night. Train was two hours and 10 minutes late. Very sorry to hear that June Ruick is no better. Give her and all the rest my best wishes. If you don't come home home soon, write.*
> *Pa,*
> *Box 144.*

The old postcard was a gift from my daughter, because of the photo, but we agreed that the message was more meaningful. I especially loved Pa's final words, "If you don't come home home soon, write." The repetition of the word "home" grabbed my heart.

I yearned to see Pa's daughter arrive at the station—but even more, to step down off that train myself and be greeted by a loving father. Instead, I grew up with a difficult dad, a man who sometimes praised me but often criticized and punished.

Over and over, I sought to resolve our conflicts, but we were estranged when he died. Years later, I understand more about his own suffering and wish we could try again. Knowing it cannot happen, I still want to be welcomed home home.

CLAIRE DE LUNE

As a child, I learned to recognize a certain melody whenever it came on the radio because my mother would announce, "That's 'Claire de Lune' by Debussy." She never told us why she loved that piece of music, and I realize I never asked.

My mother had a beautiful singing voice and majored in music at college, hoping to pursue a career as a performer. She traveled to California to seek work and had several impressive offers, but didn't take any of them.

Instead she came home to Michigan to sell shoes in a department store and sing in the church choir, where she met my father. Hearing these stories, I was glad she didn't become a singer because I wanted her to be my mother.

Now I wonder how she felt about that choice. It used to embarrass me when she sang in the kitchen in front of my friends. But when I stood next to her in church, I mouthed the words to the hymns so that I could hear her voice.

I can still hear her singing "Claire de Lune." The melody is so full of loveliness and longing, it seems to contain everything I know about my mother's life, and everything I don't know.

RAIN CHANGING TO SNOW

Rain changing to snow in the forecast. Two doors down, a young man hauls a roll of carpet out of the house. Virginia's house, I think, but not anymore. She died last summer at age 88 and a young couple has bought it. Their first house.

A slim woman staggers out onto the porch under another roll of carpet and hands it up to the young man who has backed a pick-up truck into the yard. He covers the carpet with a blue tarp and pulls up the hood of his jacket.

Not a good day to move, not a good season. But when it's your first house you hardly notice. It was February when my husband and I moved into a tiny place on Washington Street that needed work. We had paid more than we could afford, convinced we could fix it up ourselves.

I remember painting window frames and taking deep breaths to hold off the nausea. I had just found out I was pregnant, a fact we did not reveal at the bank closing when we listed two paychecks on the dotted line. A baby was not in our plans but I had begun to think it might be okay. Even wonderful.

For the nursery, I sewed curtains out of beach towels and my husband built a wooden cradle. We painted the walls blue and hoped for a girl. We never guessed she'd outgrow the cradle in three months. Never guessed we'd outgrow the house in five years.

Now, through Virginia's kitchen window I see a silhouette of the young couple embracing. Not Virginia's window. Rain changing to snow.

CAT PERSON

Early on a Saturday morning I was pushing my cart around a grocery store, trying not to cry. Trying not to notice the aisle of pet food where just two weeks before I had bought a bag of cat chow, not knowing my cat would get sick three days later and die soon after. I still imagined her at home in the window waiting for my return.

What I need, I thought, is to run into someone I know who's a cat person, but the store was full of strangers. Then, as I finished bagging my purchases, a woman approached and said, "Is that you?" She was a friend from years ago and gave me a hug. "How are you doing?"

I told her the truth because Cathy is a cat person. The first one I ever knew, in fact. Back then she had a black and white cat called Pookie which I thought a very silly name—until I had my own cat. A stray tiger I named Clara but often called Tootles, who took over my favorite rocking chair and my life. That was three cats ago, three silly names ago.

This morning Cathy and I stood beside the check-out lane and wiped away tears. "I love them more than people," she whispered and I nodded.

It was what I most needed. Next to my cat.

Leaving Home

It began with me sleeping overnight at my grandparents' house. They lived close by, so it didn't feel like being away, or not very far away. The next step was sleeping overnight at my best friend's. Everything about Bonnie's house was different: late bedtime, unlimited candy, noisy furnace.

Then there was summer camp which was two weeks of sleeping on a metal bunk in a cabin with eleven other girls. I was homesick, but I also had a glimpse of freedom. And when I left for college, I was finally *living* away from home—with all the new people and experiences and choices.

After graduation, I took a job on the East Coast, then moved to the West Coast. But whenever I was lonely, I could go home to Mom and Dad. Even after I was married, we went "home for the holidays" to my parents' house.

They were always there until suddenly they were gone, my mother dying when I was 31 and my father ten years later. Looking back, I see how I was always preparing to leave my parents, never preparing to have them leave me.

If they were here, they'd probably say, "That's how it's supposed to be."

But they're gone.

CLOSER TO THE FIRE

It is late in the fall to be camping. Darkness comes early and brings a creeping chill that penetrates my cotton sweatshirt. I pull up the hood and lean closer to the campfire. My husband grabs another piece of wood and lays it across the glowing logs.

"This oak burns real nice," he says. "Smells good, too." He turns to me. "Say, are you warm enough?"

"Almost." I stuff my hands into my pockets.

We have set up our tent on the shore of Lake Superior in Michigan's Upper Peninsula. A sharp wind comes off the water, but the chill I feel isn't just the weather. Maybe it's the season of the year or the season of my life. I feel cold and old and worn-out, like my sweatshirt with holes in the elbows.

Camping used to be easier. It used to seem like an adventure to cook outdoors and sleep on the ground. These days, the fun doesn't always offset the dirt and the rain and the toilet down the road. But the issue isn't camping, really. It's aging. It's figuring out how to let go and hang on at the same time.

"How do you know when to give it up?" I start to ask, and stop.

The oak log sighs and breaks in half, falling into the coals. There, its charred pieces begin to burn again. I take this as a good sign.

BLUE RUG

Beneath my dining room table is a big rug in many shades of blue. It's hand-made with thick cotton yarn which gives it a delicious texture—for both eye and foot, especially a bare foot. I commissioned a good friend to weave this rug for me over twenty-five years ago.

You'd never know it. The colors are bright and the shape true. And every time I wash it, I'm stunned by how handsome it looks— better than new for having a kind of lived-on look, softer and warmer.

The ultimate test has come with my current cat who has made of this rug a scratchpad and hideout, rolling up in a corner of it. Big Blue is unfazed and unfrayed.

Whatever I paid for this rug (and it seemed extravagant at the time) has been repaid in countless ways. So beautiful and durable, it gives me pleasure every day. More than pleasure, it reminds me of my friend and her remarkable skill.

When I think of things I've made—all the pots of soup and these weekly essays—they seem ephemeral by comparison. How grand it would be to create something—*to be someone*—as lovely and sturdy and useful as the blue rug.

QUITTING

My mother was in the hospital with internal bleeding. "They say I have liver trouble from drinking," she said in a puzzled voice. "Maybe it was those piña coladas I had on the cruise."

I knew it wasn't the piña coladas. Twenty years earlier, as a young girl, I had asked my mother about the wine in the cupboard that disappeared so quickly. My father told me not to mention it again.

Now the doctor was speaking to my father and me in the hallway. Her liver was too damaged to repair itself and we could only make her comfortable. We walked out to the parking lot together where my father opened the trunk of his car. It was full of empty wine bottles.

"She told me she had stopped!" he yelled, "Why didn't she stop?"

I shook my head. My mother and I had only spoken once about why she started. It was during World War II when my father was in the South Pacific and her mother had said, "Have a glass of wine. It will relax you."

She didn't know how to stop. A support group wasn't an option in her world; neither was counseling. It took me a long time to feel compassion instead of anger. To forgive her, to forgive all of us.

THERE OUGHTA BE A LAW

"There oughta be a law," I say, "businesses that go out of business ought to take their signs down." My husband nods, keeping his eye on the road as we head north for a weekend trip.

"There oughta be a law."

Instead, there are signs announcing a craft shop or restaurant or motel that no longer exists. It makes me mad and it makes me sad. We pass a farm market that's been closed for years while its big sign keeps inviting travelers to stop in. "Tomatoes, sweet corn, homemade pies!"

"When things are gone, they ought to be gone," I say, and finally hear myself.

I'm not just talking about signs but about everything that ends, that doesn't work out. Not only businesses but friendships, marriages, jobs. Plans that fall apart but leave their signs around. Failure is messy and painful—and I don't want to be reminded.

"I could use a cup of coffee and something to eat," my husband says. "How about that place up ahead?" The sign is ugly but lit up with bright red neon and I feel strangely cheered.

"FOOD," the sign reads, and we pull into the parking lot.

Ungodly Hour

"I have to get up at some ungodly hour," I say, describing a flight I need to catch.

It's only later that I wonder about that phrase. What could an "ungodly hour" be, after all? Who would believe in a God that kept hours, that wasn't available 24/7? I especially want God to be available when I'm flying. Because even though planes launch me into God-territory, I don't feel one bit more secure.

Which suggests that maybe I'm not a "true believer." There's another interesting phrase. Why do we need to say "true believer"? Who would ever want to be a "false believer"?

Certainly my concept of God has changed from the bearded man in the sky that I learned about in Sunday school. I like it that he's in the sky, especially when I'm flying, but not that he's a he.

My 24/7 God has to be bigger than gender, bigger than any of our differences. That's one of the benefits of being sky-high. Anyone who's been in a plane knows that national boundaries aren't visible from the air or religious boundaries or any other kind.

In fact, everything looks beautiful from up there. Which is why it's worth getting up at some ungodly hour. Worth believing there is no such thing.

LOOKING BACK

"The first time I saw your mother," my father liked to say, "I knew I was going to marry her.'" He was sitting in church choir at the time and my mother was coming in late to practice. Late on purpose so that she would be noticed. It was a fairytale beginning, my parents' marriage.

A couple years later they had a baby girl and then my father went off to war. He was on an aircraft carrier in the South Pacific for three years before he wrote my mother that they were heading for the "Elysian Fields."

"I snuck that one past the censors," he liked to say, "because the Elysian Fields meant paradise in Greek mythology." It must have seemed like paradise to come home safe from war to his wife and daughter. Soon they had a baby boy and a new bungalow.

It should have been happily ever after but instead, my mother was drinking and my father was angry and there were always problems with money. And I wonder, if something ends badly, was it a mistake from the beginning? Unhappy endings have a way of casting a long shadow backwards.

"I would never have left your mother," my father said after she died but I know he sometimes wanted to.

"Tell me about how you met," I said. "I like that story."

SECURITY BLANKET

I probably shouldn't admit this, but I have a security blanket.
I suspect that most of us do. Our parents may have taken away
the old flannel rag we carried around and slept with, but we found
some kind of substitute.

It might be corn chips or ice cream or a ratty old sweatshirt, but
now that we're grown up nobody can take it away. For me, my
security blanket is, well, a blanket. Call it arrested development,
but don't take it away.

When I was a little girl, I had a blue wool blanket with satin trim.
As I was falling asleep, I would run my fingers along that smooth,
cool satin and feel safe under the weight of wool.

My mother replaced the satin trim twice and then I left for college,
embarrassed to take the blanket with me. Years later, I had a
daughter of my own who found security in stuffed animals. I told
Sara about my blue blanket and she asked, "Why don't you get
another one?"

I said I was too old. Then, in junior high, she took a sewing class
and made me a small blue blanket with satin trim.

That was many years ago and I still have it, always near me on the
bed. I could tell you it keeps me warm but lots of things can keep
me warm. Security is something else.

SECTION 3:

GRADUAL CLEARING

A PLACE FOR MYSELF

During my first year at a university, I lived in a single room in the dorm. The girls on my hall were fun, but at the end of the day I needed my own space where I could do my homework and play my Frank Sinatra albums.

Still, when the opportunity came to pledge a sorority, I seized it. I thought it was a chance to change my shy, serious self into one of those popular girls—the ones who were gregarious and social and attractive to boys. My friends thought I was crazy.

But I ignored their warnings and moved into the sorority house where I had two lively roommates who stayed up late every night. I was up late, too, but not at parties. I couldn't sleep, consumed by anxiety and afraid of flunking out. How could I have made such a terrible mistake?

I thought I could change myself by some kind of osmosis, as if by being adjacent to people who were different than I was, I could become them. It didn't work, of course. I eventually made a place for myself in the sorority house, but I'm still that same shy, serious person who was never one of the popular girls.

And it's okay, really. Most of the time.

Fixing the House

There's an old gray house in my neighborhood that I walk past every week. Pink insulation sticks out where the asphalt shingles are missing. The people who lived there tore off the screen door and hauled a washer onto the lawn before they finally moved out.

After that, the house sat empty for a long time but I never saw a "For Sale" sign. "It has possibilities," I thought, sounding like a realtor. But I knew it was more than a "fixer-upper." It was a "starter-over."

Even so, it had a nice back yard and a red pine tree next to the front porch. A year passed, maybe two, and then things started changing, mostly on weekends: a new roof, new windows.

None of it happened quickly but every time I walked by, I noticed some small improvement, evidence that the owners—whoever they were—hadn't given up. And now, at last, they've moved in! The repairs aren't complete but there's a gas grill in the yard instead of a washer, and the lights are on at night.

I don't even know these new neighbors, but their efforts have touched me, reminded me how doing something good helps everybody.

CARROTS

I am late getting home from class and my husband has already started supper. As we drink a beer at the kitchen table, I hear a lid rattling on the stove. "Should you turn the carrots down?" I ask, and Dick runs to turn off the burner.

Carrots are stuck to the bottom of the pan and I am reminded of another cooking experience. "When my mother started working full-time, she would ask me to get dinner ready," I told Dick. "Once, I was cooking green beans and burned them black."

"What did she say?" he asks.

"She said, 'I've burned lots of beans; let's have carrots instead.'"

"Pretty nice of her," Dick says.

"Especially since I burned the carrots, too."

Now, the taste of burned carrots makes me happy, remembering my mother. Although she could be strict about many things, she could sometimes surprise me with her tenderness.

As a little girl, I tried to make a bird bath out of her favorite glass cooking dish and dropped it on the cement sidewalk. I was sobbing when I carried the shards into the house, but there was no spanking.

"You didn't do it on purpose," she said. "I used to get spanked for spilling milk, but nobody spills milk on purpose."

Or burns carrots.

RE-READING A BOOK

The only thing better than reading a wonderful book is re-reading it. Sure, there are plenty of good books I haven't even read once, but a new book is a risk while an old one is a comfort. So I pull Wallace Stegner's novel, *Angle of Repose*, off my shelf. I can't remember how many times I've read it, but I vividly recall the first time.

I was nine months pregnant and signing up for a college course in American Literature. The woman behind the desk gazed at my enormous belly and asked if I was sure.

We had to read ten novels in ten weeks, so I always had a book next to the rocking chair where I nursed my infant daughter. Day and night, every hour or half hour, we would be there together— Sara and me and the Great American Writers.

In *Angle of Repose*, a college professor tells the story of his artist grandmother who follows her husband west in the 1870s. Since the narrator already knows how it turns out, he doesn't have to hurry but can savor the details, ponder the meanings.

Which is the way to re-read a wonderful book. Also the way to *live* your *life*.

SAYING HELLO

I am leaving a store when I notice the woman in front of me. There is something familiar in her walk and then I know who she is—a friend from long ago.

I should say hello but I'm in a hurry. She's probably in a hurry, too, and there's no need to bother. She hasn't seen me yet and I can let it go. We're out the door now and suddenly I change my mind. "Linda," I say, and she turns around.

"Karen!"

We hug each other and stand in the sunshine to exchange greetings. But even though she's smiling, I see something else in her face and she confides that her husband moved out a year ago. I am stunned.

She and Jerry had one of those enduring marriages I've always admired, always envied. And before I can even respond, she tells me her brother has just died and her daughter moved away. "You've been through a lot," I say.

"It was a long winter," she says. "Don't you think it was a long winter?"

We talk for twenty minutes, more than we've talked in years, more than she's ever talked to me before. And I think about how I almost didn't say hello.

"Let's get together," I say, and hug her again.

CLAY FEET

On the first night of the writers conference, a famous poet stood at the podium. Witty and eloquent, he spoke about writing as a sacred calling. "Art makes the mystery of life deeper," he said, and we all nodded.

Then he picked up his new book to read his glorious poems, and the one that knocked me out was about his wife. Such love, such devotion! Ah, to have a husband who wrote you poems like that. I bought three books.

The next morning I went for an early walk and noticed the famous poet jogging with a group of young women. One of them was my roommate. "I'm having a drink with him tonight," she told me, and didn't come home until dawn.

"But that poem about his wife!" I said. Could I still admire the poems if I'd lost respect for the poet?

My roommate said I was hopelessly naïve and maybe she was right. But it took me a long time before I could read those poems again, before I could accept that my hero was a complex and flawed human being. Just like me.

"Art makes the mystery of life deeper," the poet had said. He was right.

B&B Roundup

"Can you recommend a restaurant?" I ask the woman behind the desk. "Someplace we can get a cold beer?" My husband and I stand in the lobby of a cheap motel at the western edge of Iowa, after a 500-mile drive in 90-degree heat.

"The B&B Roundup, down Main Street, on your right," she says.

We keep our eyes open for a bunch of cars out front but discover that the regulars are parked in back. The bartender looks about fifteen but knows her way around the drinks and the drinkers. The beer is very cold and I begin to think I might be able to do another 500 miles tomorrow.

Finally we order a couple of salads. "We make our own ranch dressing," the bartender says. "With buttermilk, every day." The dressing tastes fresher than the lettuce, but I don't mind. There are hot biscuits in a plastic basket.

A pair of horns from a longhorn steer hangs above the bar, along with a drift of smoke from hamburgers on the grill. People are wrong when they say that places in America are losing their regional differences. Where I live, we tend to put moose heads on the wall, but it's the same kind of place. One-of-a-kind place.

Nobody could franchise these local hang-outs. It makes travel worth the effort and home more like home. True, there's fast food everywhere but there are B&B Roundups everywhere, too.

The locals know where they are, and we park in back.

GOOD PUPPY

When I was twelve years old, I was finally allowed to get a puppy and my father charged me with full responsibility for her care. "You won't ever see me walking a dog!" he said.

She was six weeks old, a black-and-white cocker spaniel I named Cindy. The early days were hard, especially the nights when she whined nonstop despite the ticking clock and hot water bottle we tucked in alongside her.

But she settled in and became my devoted companion, sprinting upstairs every morning to wake me and waiting at the window after school. In the evenings, I took her for walks around the block so she could chase the squirrels and sniff every tree trunk.

It wasn't long, however, before I was going off to college and leaving Cindy behind. I knew she would get good care but worried she might be lonely. Coming home for the holidays, I was surprised to find Cindy on my father's lap while he watched television.

Each night after dinner, he snapped on the leash and took her for a walk around the block.

And years later, when Cindy was too ill to walk, it was my father who lifted her into the car and took her to the vet to be put down.

"She's a good puppy," he said.

Memorial Day

It's Memorial Day and I'm visiting my parents' graves at Oakwood Cemetery, a lovely scene of well-kept lawns and ancient trees. Many families are here, and single people, older people—lifting flowers out of cars, enacting private rituals of remembrance.

I sit on the grass and talk quietly with the two people whom I dearly miss despite our various conflicts. My father's simple bronze plaque identifies him as a Lieutenant Commander, U.S. Navy, World War II. And next to the stone is an American flag, as there is on every veteran's grave today.

Hundreds and hundreds of flags in every direction across the vast cemetery, testimony to the immense cost of wars and the price paid by the dead and the living. I'm always moved to see these flags. Who puts them out every year?

So I asked the sexton at the cemetery office. "Seventeen hundred flags," he said. "It's done by volunteers from veterans groups, church groups, state and local police." Without fanfare or recognition, they perform this service, and if asked, would probably say, "Because it's the right thing to do." So would the veterans.

These silent flags speak to me, louder than any speeches, about what a privilege it is to sit here on the grass—a far cry from the many battlefields where veterans saw duty. A far cry.

CARRYING THE BAGGAGE

A friend is telling me about the new man in her life. "I really like the guy," she says, "but I'm finding out he has a lot of baggage."

"We all do by this age," I say. She and I are no longer young but not yet ready to be old. We sip our glasses of wine and reflect on that load of hang-ups and heartaches we carry around, some we're born with, others we collect over time.

"Actually, we had baggage when we were twenty," I say, "but we didn't see it then."

When I was twenty, I thought I could leave everything behind by leaving my parents' house. It took me another ten years to feel the weight of what I was dragging along. A siege of anxiety brought me to my knees and to a counselor who helped me identify my baggage and claim it.

"You weren't loved enough as a child," he said. "Most people aren't loved enough." I knew our family had problems but I thought I had managed to escape, to reinvent myself.

My friend pours us more wine and I pick up my glass.

"Maybe the baggage itself isn't the problem," I say, "but whether or not you've unpacked it. You've got to decide what to keep and what to let go of."

"I want a smaller bag," she says. "A carry-on."

HOME FOR CHRISTMAS

I've been looking forward to this for weeks, being home for Christmas. Now I'm here, tucked under the familiar blue wool blanket—and wide awake at two a.m. I was sure that when I could "sleep in my own bed" I could sleep, but the insomnia that has stalked me at college has followed me here. Finally, at four a.m., I crawl out of bed and tiptoe into my parents' room.

"Mom," I whisper, touching her shoulder. "I can't sleep."

She is instantly alert. "I'm glad you woke me up," she says quietly. "I was hungry and I didn't know it."

Soon we are sitting on the couch by the light of the Christmas tree, drinking tea and eating frosted Santa Clauses. Actually, she is eating and I am crying, telling her about everything that has gone wrong this past semester.

"It was a terrible mistake," I sob, "moving into a sorority house. It's so noisy and I can't study and I can't sleep." My mother nods, sipping her tea.

"We'll figure it out," she says.

Looking back, I see that my worst moment was her finest hour. Not when she helped me figure it out but when she said, "I was hungry and I didn't know it."

Rental

When I left my first marriage, I moved into a small rental house with my ten-year-old daughter. The floors creaked and the windows leaked and the oven door wouldn't close—but I loved the place. It felt cozy and funky and just the right size for my downsized life.

Then, after I'd lived there about six months, my landlord stopped by to tell me he had a buyer for the house. "But I like it here," I said, "and I'm in the middle of a divorce."

Dan and I sat on the grass in the back yard and talked awhile and finally he stood up. "I went through a divorce," he said. "I won't sell the house."

I stayed for five years, and figured out how to keep the oven door closed with a hanger and a rubber band. Also how to be a single mom, a single woman. I grappled with guilt and grief and unintended consequences—losing extended family, people taking sides. A roller-coaster, a slog.

And if something went wrong with the house, I called my landlord. When he had to retrieve my pantyhose from the bathtub drain, Dan laughed and said, "Not hard enough."

When the birds in the attic turned out to be a battery in the smoke detector, he said, "Not hard enough."

When a stray cat came to our back porch and my daughter wanted to keep it, he changed the rule about "No Pets."

After we moved out, Dan sold the house. I still drive by. There's a stroller out front these days and a pot of red geraniums.

ASYMMETRY

A big silver maple lives a couple blocks from me, taller than any house on the street. Staring up, I notice how crooked the tree is, how unbalanced where its branches have been chopped off. Year after year, the city crews have trimmed it to make room for power lines.

My neighborhood is full of such trees—maples and oaks that have survived generations of hand saws and chain saws. Stripped of their symmetry, these trees find another way to be beautiful. And now, as spring arrives, their remaining branches are fat with buds. Soon they will be thick with leaves, reaching across the streets in canopies of shade.

Bicycling past them, I admire these old trees and wish I were as forgiving as they are, as resilient. Wish I could accept, as gracefully as they do, awkward transformations.

Few of us reach maturity without getting trimmed, without losing parts of ourselves. Nobody asks our permission before they arrive with their saws and leave us lopsided.

Sometimes it's hard to keep my balance. To keep believing I have something to offer, a reason to keep going and growing, season after season. Like the old trees that leaf out, with whatever they have left.

CORRECTIONS

I was first attracted to my husband because he knew things I didn't know. His background was science while I was an English major. Dick was an outdoor person while I had never ventured into the wilderness.

Other people get acquainted over coffee; we were in a canoe. Dick handed me a paddle and demonstrated how to dip, pull, lift, twist. It wasn't as easy as he made it look, but between strokes, I learned about otters and ospreys and bald eagles.

Dick was curious about my world, too—accepting my offer of novels and poetry with good grace. We even taught a class on backpacking and journal-keeping. I think the backpacking part was more successful.

Still, we were pretty sure this relationship would endure and decided to buy a house together. After a long search, I found one I thought might work, especially since it had so many beautiful trees. Surely that would please my nature-loving companion. But after I exclaimed for a third time about the pine trees, he said quietly, "They're *spruce* trees."

Of course I was grateful for this information—but it's never easy to be corrected, even if you're incorrect. Especially then.

HIGHLANDS

As soon as I got off the plane in Glasgow, Scotland, I felt at home, although I'd never been there. The ruddy, angular faces and thick accents seemed familiar somehow.

Half-Scottish on my mother's side, I yearned to know this place my grandfather had left and longed for. So when I finished college, I accepted an invitation to visit my friend, Betty, who was spending the summer in the highlands.

Betty was waitressing at the Olgivie Arms Hotel but I couldn't afford a room there, so slept in a tent provided by her boyfriend, Jock McBride, the red-bearded, blue-eyed Pony-Man who had stolen her heart and could have had mine for the asking.

The next morning, Jock took a group of us pony-trekking and as we rode up into the rugged mountains—the mist lifting and the sheep calling—I knew I belonged to this lovely, melancholy landscape. To this ancient country with its defeats and defiance echoing down the valleys like the wail of bagpipes.

Stopping for lunch, we unsaddled the horses and stretched out in the sun. Jock passed around a pint of whisky and grinned at me. "Enjaying yersilf, Karr'n?" he asked.

"Oh, yes. *Och, aye.*"

Matching Ottoman

A friend bought a house in an auction and decided to sell all the furniture.

"Do you have any overstuffed chairs?" I asked.

"I have overstuffed everything," she said. And there it was, an enormous old horsehair chair that was just the sort of thing my daughter could curl up in with a book.

"A steal at seventy-five dollars," my friend said. "And the matching ottoman is only fifty."

I sat in the chair, stroking its great round arms and admiring its carved wooden legs. The footstool was equally handsome, but I didn't have an extra fifty dollars.

"I'll take the chair," I said.

My daughter spent many hours in the horsehair chair, and then went off to college, leaving it for me. Now I'm the one who curls up with a book and my only regret is that I didn't buy the ottoman.

It was a false economy, saving fifty dollars and losing something I could never replace. I can see the missing ottoman so clearly—the way I can see other things I've lost that often seem more vivid and valuable than the things I have. That metallic blue Mustang, for example, that I gave up in favor of a sensible sedan. The brooding novelist I met at a conference and never forgot.

Someone else is resting their feet on that ottoman now. Do they wish they had the matching chair?

Gradual Clearing

Under a gray sky, we load the canoe onto the truck, choosing to believe the forecast: "becoming partly sunny." But the gloomy weather suits my mood.

"You okay?" my husband asks.

"I feel sort of depressed," I say.

The wind is sharp as we push off into the Manistee River and I wish I'd worn long underwear. On this late fall day, the water is low but the colors are high. Red and orange and yellow, the oaks and maples stand along the bluffs, shining with their own light.

"Let's stop on that island for coffee," Dick says, and we sit on a birch log to open the thermos. I hold the steaming cup close to my face and munch a piece of molasses cookie.

"No sun yet," I say.

"I'm still glad we came," he says.

Back in the canoe, I tie my bonnet under my chin. Around the next bend I see a brilliant red maple leaning far out over the river—the river that will eventually claim its life but now reflects its beauty. I want to have the courage to lean out over my death, I think. Over my life. To risk believing I am valuable and I belong. Right here, right now.

It's mostly cloudy when we end our trip four hours later. As I look up, searching for blue, I feel a pleasant ache in my shoulders.

"How are you doing?" my husband asks.

"Gradual clearing," I say.

TOGETHERNESS

The way my husband fixes his breakfast toast has begun to annoy me. "You could save time if you toasted the second two pieces while you're buttering the first two," I tell him.

"I'm not trying to save time," he says.

He also uses too much jam. Who needs so much jam? And who is this *shrew* inside my head? Hearing her familiar voice, I know it is definitely time. In fact, it is past time for my husband and me to enjoy a few days apart.

Marriage is the hardest relationship in the world, I think. Being a parent isn't easy but the whole goal is to separate, for the child to grow up and leave.

The goal of a marriage is to grow up and *stay*. But sometimes the secret of staying is leaving for a little while. That's why I'm alert to the toast factor. When I start feeling annoyed by the way my husband eats his breakfast—or breathes in and out—I know it's time for some space.

Fortunately, he is planning a trip. And almost as soon as he is out of the driveway, I can feel myself falling in love again. A feeling I want to enjoy by myself for a few days.

SACRED COWS

Just before our plane landed in Kathmandu, Nepal, we filled out a questionnaire about the purpose of our visit. I checked the box next to "Trekking" but I wanted to check "Pilgrimage."

Exploring the city the next day, I noticed bales of hay on the street corners. Then I saw the cows for whom the hay had been provided. They wandered around at will, poking their heads into shops and disrupting traffic.

As a Westerner, I had heard about the Hindu belief in "sacred cows" and thought the whole idea rather strange and certainly unhygienic. Now I was sharing a sidewalk with them. Now I was watching a lovely woman in a lavender sari touch the side of a cow and touch her forehead in reverence. I could feel something shift in the baggage of my assumptions.

Growing up a Christian, I was taught to look for holy things in church, not roaming my neighborhood on four legs. But suddenly it began to make sense that the divine should appear as an ordinary beast—everywhere present and accessible, to be touched and tended. Not one incarnation many years ago, but thousands of them, here and now.

A pilgrimage was a journey to a sacred place—to this dusty, crowded place where the local people greeted us by bowing their heads, hands in prayer, saying, "Namaste." Our guide translated: "I salute the god in you."

I had come to Nepal hoping to glimpse a spiritual tradition outside my own—and here it was. The divine within reach, within me.

Friends with History

The first time Judy and I had lunch, we spoke from the heart. She was just re-entering the workforce after raising four kids; I was just exiting to have one. But we didn't talk much about children.

We talked about ourselves, asking hard questions. Judy was wondering about leaving her marriage. I was wondering about leaving my job. We didn't know what we wanted, except to become better friends. That was over forty years ago and we're still talking.

Even though she moved to New Jersey and then to Arizona. Even though we've been through divorces and remarriages, through deaths and births and re-births. Not without conflicts along the way. I've let her down; she's hurt my feelings, but we never gave up on each other.

Now the hard questions are about life and death. Judy's husband died recently and she's living in a retirement community where I visited her. How lovely it was to jump right in without having to explain who anybody was. Who we are. Our lives have changed but not our need to share them with someone we've known over time—especially as time is running out.

"I'm not coming to be a tourist," I told her, "but to sit in your living room with wine and conversation." And so we did.

CIVILITY

When I was growing up, my mother always wore a dress, a housedress for housework and something nicer when she went out. Women wore hats, too, and so did men—hats with brims—and men took off their hats indoors.

Things were different for children, as well. When adults came into the room, we were expected to stand up. And we addressed them as Mr. and Mrs., not by their first names. Another formality, strictly enforced in my home, was writing thank you notes. Even before I could write, I learned to print the words, "Thank You."

Well, the world is a different place today—vastly more informal—and I'm grateful for much of it. I like wearing pants but I miss receiving thank you notes, not only as an expression of gratitude, but of acknowledgement. Thank you for the gift and for the connection we share. It seems as if common courtesy isn't so common anymore.

Because it's not just about manners. It's about respect. Respect for self and respect for others—the foundation of a functioning society. We can agree to disagree, but only if we're talking to each other and also listening. Reminding ourselves that we're all just muddling through our days, our lives.

Please. Thank you. You're welcome.

BLAME ME

"Maybe I wasn't the greatest mom," I say, "but I must have done a few things right."

"None," my daughter says, grinning. We are sitting at the kitchen table, drinking coffee and catching up. Sara is married now and working two jobs, so we grab whatever time we can to be together.

"Maybe there was one thing," she says, and I wonder what it could be. Hoping she might say how much she appreciates the way I read her books or helped with homework.

"You said I could blame you," she says. "Remember?"

"Remind me."

"You told me that if I didn't want to do something, like stay out late or go somewhere with a bunch of friends, I could always say, 'My mom won't let me.' That really came in handy."

I know what she means. My parents always set an early curfew, and I was often grateful for the excuse to get home. Then when I was a senior in college, we could get keys to the residence hall and suddenly there was no curfew. Sometimes I said I didn't have a key. I had discovered that freedom is more free with limits.

"Well, I'm glad I did something right," I tell Sara. "Feel free to blame me anytime."

"I do," she says.

FORGIVING MY FATHER

"On the way to the hospital, we didn't have a name picked out for a girl," my father liked say. "We were so sure it was going to be a boy."

I spent my life trying to make up the difference, trying to prove I was valuable.

"Why only one A?" he asked after my first year at college. When I got straight A's, he complained that I was "too intellectual." And always, "too thin."

I should have realized he was impossible to please, but parents are powerful. If he didn't love me, how could anyone else love me? The last time I saw him he recited his familiar criticisms, adding that I'd ruined my daughter's life by getting divorced.

"I don't deserve this," I said.

"I'm just telling you for your own good," he said.

He died soon afterwards of heart failure which didn't surprise me. He left me out of his will which shouldn't have surprised me either. *Unforgivable*, I told myself, but anger finally wore me out. I wanted to forgive him but I couldn't get there.

Months later I was watching home movies and, in one brief scene, saw my mother looking tense, my father terribly thin. World War II had just ended and he had returned from the South Pacific, only to be diagnosed with a serious illness. In his gaunt face I saw so much fear.

For the first time, I felt compassion. Forgiveness might be within reach.

TURTLES IN THE SUN

Before the snow melts from the woods, before the buds swell on the branches, my husband and I drag our canoe into the river. Bundled in layers, we paddle hard to warm up, lifting our faces to the sun.

We aren't the only ones. On logs along the river's edge, turtles lift their faces to the sun, too—soaking up the pale yellow light. I nod at these fellow creatures but they dive into the water at our approach, except for one who holds his ground to watch us float by.

"Welcome back," I say quietly. "Good to see you."

The last time I glimpsed turtles was late fall—on the same logs, soaking up the slanting rays of golden light, storing it up for the long cold months ahead. Turtles are in tune with the seasons in a way I will never be because their lives depend on it.

My life depends on other things—family, friends, work, play. I am insulated from the seasons by a snug house, a grocery store, a car. Nature as scenery, not habitat.

The turtles, however, are at home out here—rain or shine or under ice. Survival is serious business but it's not all business. There's pleasure, too. And I wonder which they enjoy more: the last warmth of fall or the first warmth of spring?

I can't decide either.

START AT THE BOTTOM

When I moved to Traverse City in 1970, I had a master's degree and years of experience, but I couldn't find a job. Desperate to pay the rent, I followed up on a "Gal Friday" position at the local newspaper.

Nobody would use that term today, but back then it described a kind of all-purpose assistant on the bottom rung of the organization. "Reading proofs, delivering proofs," the advertising director told me. "You're overqualified." Yes, but I needed the work.

Turns out, I also loved the work, the newspaper business—making friends with the typesetters and the merchants. Soon, I was hassling the publisher to let me write book reviews. "Okay, write a couple and I'll have a look," he said. A few months later, he invited me to write a personal column.

Meanwhile, I got married and then left the newspaper to have a baby, but I kept writing my weekly column for thirty years. When my daughter was in school, I decided to re-enter the workforce and started at the bottom again, filling in for somebody at the college who was on maternity leave. By the time she came back, I had earned my own job.

So, my career advice is to start at the bottom. If you're good, you'll move up fast—and you'll know *everything*.

TREATS

My husband and my cat are waiting up when I get home. I am late and know my husband has been worried. As for my cat, I see no evidence that she ever worries about anything.

No, she has waited up because we have an evening ritual. I throw her some cat treats which she likes to chase. My veterinarian said they help remove tartar.

"You must have had a good time," my husband says.

"The food was wonderful," I say and shake out the treats while I tell him about my evening. "Mary has met somebody on the Internet."

The cat meows and I throw a few treats. "They sound like soul mates," I continue, and grab the vitamins I usually take at dinner. The cat meows again but the treats are gone.

"Egad," I shriek, "I just took a cat treat instead of my calcium!" My husband thinks this is the funniest thing he's ever heard and I do, too, except that it happened to me. "I don't dare read the ingredients," I say.

"You're probably protected from fleas and hairballs," he says.

"And if I'd chewed it first, it would remove tartar."

TELL ME

My mother loved Christmas. The decorating began early and covered every available surface: holly on the banister, stockings on the mantel, candles on the tables. My father used to joke that the electric bill went down because we lit the house with candles.

She baked, too, and I helped. First, there were little loaves of cranberry and pumpkin bread, plus small fruitcakes, which we gave as gifts. Next were the endless batches of sugar cookies—cut into stars, reindeer, snowmen, Santas—and elaborately decorated. I made myself sick on frosting.

The gifts were gorgeously wrapped and too generous. There was no stopping my mother at Christmas. We gave up trying.

I miss my mother, especially during the holiday season. She died at age sixty-one and I've lived most of my life without her. She was an insecure and immature woman who drank too much, spent too much, died too young. And I miss her.

So, what I most want for Christmas is for someone to say, "Tell me about your mom."

It might be the gift everyone is waiting for, that invitation: "Tell me about your mom or your dad or your childhood Christmases—anything. Just *tell* me."

WELL-HUNG DOOR

I live in an old house, and there are some nice things about old houses. Nooks and crannies, history and character. There are also other things, many of which appear on a list called "Improvements."

Last summer, it was a new back door. The old door was here when my husband and I bought the house over twenty years ago. It had huge claw marks in the wood as if the *Hound of the Baskervilles* had been trying to get in.

Clearly, it was time to replace it, but like so much else in American life, there were too many choices. Wood, steel, fiberglass? Hardware? Storm door?

Then, when those decisions were made, there was the old-house factor: nothing was square. Except, of course, the new door. So we were grateful to have a carpenter who knew the ins and outs, you might say, of creating a functional door in a dysfunctional space.

A high-traffic space that's in use every day, four seasons of the year. No small thing, this rectangle of elegance and precision. The smooth glide and solid thunk of that door in its frame. Tumble of locks, turn of key.

Maybe it's not rocket science. Maybe it's more important.

ICE FLOES

Ours is the only car in the parking lot on this Sunday afternoon. My husband and I walk north along the Lake Michigan shore, pulling on gloves and putting up hoods. It might be twenty degrees on the thermometer but it feels like zero.

Below zero when you factor in the wind chill that freezes my eyelashes. I swing my arms and pick up the pace. The footing is firm because the sand is frozen solid. Then, when I'm finally warm, I need to stop and dig a Kleenex out of a pocket for my runny nose.

It's a good chance to stare and listen. Strange to be on a beach and not hear waves, but they're lapping against the ice far out in the lake where white turns to dark blue against the horizon. In the silence I hear the creak of ice floes like voices in a conversation.

The sun has dazzle without warmth, a pale yellow disc in the southern sky. For a moment I wish it was summer again, that I was wading in bare feet and stepping over sand castles, dodging dogs and children.

In July, of course, I never yearn for February. We rarely prefer the harder path but sometimes—like today—I glimpse its harsh beauty.

INHERITING THE COUCH

I have an old Victorian couch which belonged to my grandparents. It has blue velvet upholstery and a curved wooden back. Although its delicate little legs look too small to support it, the couch has proved remarkably sturdy.

As a young girl, I sat on this couch with my grandfather, my feet just reaching the edge of the cushions. He read poetry to me and showed me his big books of art reproductions. The couch wasn't blue then but covered in a beige fabric that scratched my bare legs.

Years later, after my grandfather had died and my grandmother was moving out of her house, the couch was offered to me. It had shiny green tapestry upholstery and seemed to fit right into my brownstone apartment in Chicago.

Several moves and fabrics later, it sits in the living room of my old house in Traverse City, alongside furniture that is modern and colonial and everything else. When people comment on the couch, I explain its origins, adding, "It's probably not something I would pick out."

I inherited the couch, along with so much else—my brown hair and curious mind, my freckles and my fears. I might choose differently if I could. I might not.

SECTION 4:

VISIBILITY UNLIMITED

Into the Current

After so much preparation, we are finally at the river. My husband slides the canoe into the water and almost before we pick up our paddles, we are swept into the current, *gathered* in, as if into the arms of a loved one.

Dick and I have been paddling together over thirty years and he was my teacher. I remember how graceful it looked when he showed me, how awkward it felt when I tried it. Dip, pull, lift, twist in one seamless movement.

"You're a good paddler," he says now from the stern and I nod, clunking the paddle against the bow. If I think about it, I lose my rhythm. Looking down, I see how fast we're going, see leaves tumbling under water and spinning out ahead of us.

The branches of a dead tree give the river a voice, a rippling soft song. A wind roughens the surface and scatters sunlight into a thousand dancing pieces. Everything is moving, sunlight into shadow, silence into singing. During all our getting ready, the river was going and flowing, ready or not.

I look down and see how fast we're going, how thirty years have vanished like leaves tumbling and spinning away. I feel the current under the canoe, so strong that I could stop paddling if I wanted to—but I don't.

BROTHER & SISTER

Last summer, my brother took me sailing on Lake Huron near where he lives. When Bob struggled to haul up the sail, his voice held an edge of panic. "Oh, oh, this isn't good." Panic that I instantly recognized because we both tend to catastrophize.

Of course we do. We grew up in the same family where problems were often denied, rarely solved. Later, drinking a beer in his back yard, we talked about this tendency, and other issues we've dragged with us from childhood.

"You were the boy they wanted," I remind Bob.

"You got better grades," he says. We laugh about this stuff now, but old gripes and grudges have made it hard for us to be friends, have sometimes kept us estranged for months, years.

Then, we find our way back. Frayed and fraught as it is, I don't want to lose this connection. I wouldn't say we're close, but there have been moments—once when my daughter almost died and Bob showed up at the hospital. Once when he was afraid to leave on a trip and called me.

Whatever we have, I'll never have it with anyone else. Knowing Bob and I struggle with the same fears makes the struggle less lonely. "All these years can pass," he says, "but always you're there."

COMB-OVER

In a doctor's waiting room the other day, I watched a tall man walk in, a good-looking man with gray hair and a carefully-tended comb-over. My first thought was to feel sorry for him, not that he was bald, but that he needed to hide his baldness.

But my next thought was that we all have comb-overs, every single one of us. We are all hiding some kind of defect—visible or invisible, real or imagined—that we work very hard every day to disguise.

I have a scar on my right cheek, for example, from a deep cut I suffered as a child. I wore my hair long for years, parted on the left, so that my thick locks would hang over my right cheek. I'm sure I never fooled anyone.

Then, when I was thirty, I was with a group of women discussing our bodies, what we liked and disliked about them. The list of dislikes was enormous and called my attention to things in others I'd mostly never noticed, or features I'd admired for their distinctive irregularity.

In a perfect world, there would be no perfection. The bald man would know he was even more handsome without a comb-over.

KNOWING HOW

I carry my old desk lamp into the elegant lighting store, trying to slip past the crystal chandeliers on my way to the repairs department. Standing in line, I stare at a clutter of parts I can't identify. "Can I help you?" the man asks.

"I need a new switch," I say, gesturing at my old lamp. "When I turn the three-way bulb on the lowest setting, it flickers."

The man removes the shade and the bulb. "A 50-100-200-watt bulb is kind of hard on this switch," he says, "but the switch itself is fine." Then he holds the bulb up to my ear. "Listen."

I hear a strange low humming, like the sound I imagine the universe makes in deep space. "The filaments are loose," the man says. "Maybe it got bumped."

He takes a 30-70-100-watt bulb out of a package and screws it into my lamp. "You might want to try a lower wattage." And as he hands me my lamp, I realize again what it means to have really useful knowledge about the way the world works, about what goes wrong and how to fix it. To know it isn't the switch but the bulb.

I reach for my purse, but he shakes his head. "No charge."

LILACS IN BLOOM

When I see lilacs in bloom, I have to stop. Sometimes it's in the country where enormous old bushes grow beside abandoned barns. Sometimes it's in my neighborhood alleys where they grow beside garages that used to be horse stables.

These orphan bushes that nobody waters or prunes are lavish with their gifts. And I stop what I'm doing to admire the rich colors— dark purple, pale violet, purest white. I lean into the moist clusters and inhale that honey lavender smell.

Now, it's true you can buy lilac bushes at a nursery and plant them in your back yard. I have done this myself and confess the results are disappointing. The branches spindly, the blossoms spare.

Lilacs, it seems, resist cultivation and do better in forgotten places with full sun and freedom. I admire this. They speak to me of something in myself that yearns to grow wild at the edges, to flourish untended and pour out my glory for one brief moment. Maybe someone will stop, maybe not.

If you pick lilacs, they will wilt in an hour. Better to lean into the living blossoms and bury your face in fragrance.

HITCHHIKING TO STONEHENGE

Homer asked if I wanted to go to Stonehenge. "We'll have to hitch-hike," he said, so we took the London tube as far west as we could and stood in the rain with our thumbs out. A lorry driver waved and shifted his enormous semi down, down until it finally stopped and we climbed into the cab.

I sat backwards on the gearbox and admired the driver's cranberry vest, the tattoos on his forearms. "Thirty-two tons of Scotch whiskey," he said.

At Amesbury, he found us a ride to Salisbury Plain. And suddenly, there they were—the gray giants in a sacred circle, standing stones that had been standing since the dawn of time. Built to calculate the dawn of time, in fact, the return of the sun each spring solstice.

The sun had returned for us, too, and dried off the grass where we sat with cheap wine and bread. We put away our cameras and brochures. I knew there were lots of theories about the history of this prehistoric site, but I wanted to absorb its mystery first.

"Maybe we should all just worship the sun," Homer said. "It's the reason for everything. We could stop fighting and sit together on the grass."

Antique Commode

In a corner of my living room sits an antique wooden cabinet which our family has always called the "commode." It originally functioned as a washstand with an elegant marble top for a pitcher of water and a cupboard underneath for a chamber pot.

Fortunately, I grew up in a world without chamber pots, so the commode has served many other purposes. There's a story that it traveled from Scotland with my great grandfather, but no one is alive who can verify. I remember it first from the attic bedroom of the family cottage where my cousins and I used it as a vanity table to stash hairbrushes and ribbons.

When the cottage was sold, the commode was given to my mother and she kept her jewelry in the long drawer. Every evening before my father returned from work, she dressed up for his arrival and invited me to pick out her necklace and earrings.

Now, in my own house, the commode contains dishes and candles, plus a set of tiny wine glasses too delicate to use. Mostly it holds memories, mysteries about where it came from and where it will go from here.

I am reminded how our things outlast us, which I find reassuring and unsettling. One day, I will be gone and the antique commode will remain—holding, perhaps, a fragrance of candles.

CABBAGE

The green cabbage was so big, it slipped out of my hand and rolled into the carrots just as the overhead spray came on, misting the vegetables and my shirt. Finally, I wrestled the cabbage into my cart and onto the check-out counter.

"Wow, a giant," the woman said.

"Too big," I said, as a puddle formed beneath it. "And too wet."

"Blame the cabbage," she said. When our eyes met, I knew we were thinking the same thing. Thank goodness we had something *else* to blame, something as blameless as a cabbage.

Today's world seems so full of conflict and disagreement, so poisoned with animosity and blame, that we're all exhausted trying to figure out what's wrong, what's right, who's in charge, and where do we go from here?

We learned about blame early in life, of course, pinning our problems onto siblings and playmates and parents. But we're supposed to outgrow that behavior, supposed to grow up and accept responsibility. Supposed to pick up a rag and dry the counter.

"I think it's a T-shirt," the woman said. "Maybe a movement."

Blame the Cabbage!

FIRST GIFT

I still have my first gift from my first husband, on the occasion of my eighteenth birthday. It's a handsome wool sweater with uneven stripes of gray, brown, and black—and little wooden buttons down the front. I recall trying it on at a department store and deciding it was too expensive.

But my new boyfriend bought it anyway. It was the kind of gesture he liked to make—a quality of generosity. We'd only had a couple of dates and my mother worried about the appropriateness of such a gift. In a month, we were going steady.

Marriage came many years later, after college and travel and work. Somehow, the striped sweater followed me around from place to place.

Today, the cuffs are a yellowish color from a house fire we survived. Smoke damage. I almost threw it away then but decided that the stains added value. And now, I discover it again in my cedar chest. Strange, how I have hung onto the sweater even though the marriage ended. Even though I don't wear it.

Why do I keep it? Because the sweater contains more memories than all the photo albums. No smiling faces, only the soft wool in an uneven pattern. Love and hope, sadness and regret. I hold it in my arms and remember.

GALILEO

Galileo was an astronomer who lived in the early 1600s, a time when religion not only ruled the world but defined it. That definition included the "fact" that the sun and all the stars and planets revolved around the earth. It took the church a long time—long after Galileo's death—to acknowledge that his theory was correct and the sun was at the center.

Today, it's easy to think about life in the 1600s and feel superior. We know so much more now.

The Black Plague raged through Europe during Galileo's lifetime, killing half the population, and no one knew the cause. His daughter sent him a remedy made of "dried figs, nuts, rue leaves and salt," held together with honey and washed down with wine. "They say it makes a marvelous defense," she wrote.

We know so much more now, it's easy to assume we know everything. But I wonder what we believe today that will turn out to be just as false as the earth-centered world? As a remedy of figs and honey?

The church made Galileo retract his statements but they couldn't make the sun revolve around the earth. "Still it moves," Galileo said about the earth.

Still it does.

MEADOW

I stay in the tent until my husband tells me the coffee is perking. It's one of the few luxuries available out here in the woods. Slowly, I roll out of my sleeping bag and pull on cold blue jeans. Dick has built a small fire and I drag my canvas chair close to the warmth.

"Here," he says, "See if it's strong enough." I watch the steaming liquid arc into my mug and can tell it's plenty strong.

Then Dick points behind me and I turn slowly to see twin fawns scampering out of the woods into the wide meadow next to our campsite. They are so young they still have their spots and seem oblivious to our presence.

Maybe they haven't learned to be afraid of humans yet. We watch them graze and play and then—at some signal which is imperceptible to us—the fawns gallop back across the meadow and disappear into the woods.

"Their mother got worried," Dick says.

"I know the feeling," I say.

After breakfast, we dismantle the tent and load our gear into the truck. Dick has owned these wooded acres for many years but recently decided to put the property up for sale.

I stand in the meadow for a few more minutes. If I knew this was the last time, could I enjoy it more? No.

NEIGHBORS

If someone tells me he has a skunk under his porch, I am politely interested. But if that someone lives next door to me, I'm riveted. My porch might be at risk. Or my cat. Or my sleep.

Which is why I host a neighbors' potluck a couple times a year. We need to share intelligence on off-leash dogs and on-site skunks. Who's remodeling or having a baby. And when is the Light & Power Company going to activate that new pole and take down the old one?

This is about as grassroots as it gets, including conversations about lawns and mowers. Most of us aren't social friends but maybe something *harder*—friends by chance, by proximity, who share responsibility for a particular corner of the world.

We depend on each other not only for live-trapping critters and borrowing ladders but for creating a place to call home. And if there's a problem somewhere down the road, even right next door or across the alley, it's easier to solve it with somebody you already know.

My husband trimmed a neighbor's tree and received a bag of homegrown tomatoes. Now he's alert to every dead branch. When I locked myself out of my house, another neighbor offered to help me break in. When that failed, he offered me a martini.

Thank goodness for neighbors and potlucks. It's time to swap stories about oak wilt and pot holes and garage sales. Everybody knows the drill: a dish to pass and a lawn chair.

DRYING DISHES

My father wasn't much of a cook but he always washed the dinner dishes and took pride in his work. It was my job to dry and put them away.

Sometimes we listened to the ball game on the radio and other times we talked about my homework. One night, I noticed a plate with some food on it and handed it back to him.

"What's the problem?" he asked.

"You didn't get it clean," I said.

"A good drier never finds food on a plate," he said.

What he meant was if food got left on a plate, a good drier wiped it off without saying anything. This seemed dishonest to me and I wanted to say so, but I just kept picking up the dishes and listening to the ballgame.

This was many years ago now, but recently I was drying dishes for my husband and found a plate with some food on it. I almost handed it back and then heard my father's voice saying, "A good drier never finds food on a plate."

I had lived long enough to know this rule wasn't about honesty; it was about kindness. And it wasn't about dishes, either.

Her Name

In college, I dated a guy named Hank who was a witty fellow with a gift for language. Although the romance didn't last, some of his droll observations have lingered. Once he remarked, "I've had a lot of one-night stands with Truth, but in the morning I can never remember her name."

It was funny, of course, but I guessed it was also accurate. Now, all these years later, I can verify encounters of my own, moments of such clarity I was sure I'd uncovered the meaning of life. Then, the next day, it was gone.

Some years ago while in London, I stood on Westminster Bridge remembering Wordsworth's sonnet composed in the same place in 1802:

> This city now doth, like a garment, wear
> The beauty of the morning ...
> Ne'er saw I, never felt a calm so deep.
> (Lines 4, 5, 11)

I, too, had a sense of profound well-being—as if I had arrived where I was supposed to be and was in the presence of truth. When I returned to my hotel, however, I couldn't describe what I'd experienced to friends. The feeling remained but the wisdom had dissolved.

I remembered Hank's throw-away line that I didn't throw away. A line he has no doubt forgotten and I am still grateful for. This is how we shape each other's lives and never know. Never remember her name.

BLACK COFFEE

In my family, dinner ended with the children being excused to go play while the parents and grandparents stayed at the table to drink coffee and talk. At first, I was eager to leave but as I got older, I yearned to stay and listen.

When I was finally invited to join the adults (somewhere in adolescence) I discovered the price of admission. If I drank half my milk, I could fill the glass with coffee. What a privilege! And what an awful taste!

I tried to sip with nonchalance but secretly wondered why anyone could prefer this bitter dark liquid to a can of cold pop? Maybe growing up wasn't such a great thing.

I thought being an adult meant doing anything you wanted, having all the power and all the freedom. Instead, I heard them worrying about taxes and illness, politics and war. Still, I stayed at the table and got used to the taste. Today I drink it as hot and black as I can get it.

And I've decided that being an adult is a little like drinking coffee—dark and bitter at times. Even so, a privilege.

LIVE MUSIC

After camping in the rain for three days, we decided to go into town for supper. The town was Munising, in Michigan's Upper Peninsula, and the restaurant was the Falling Rock Café & Bookstore. All we wanted was a dry place and some good food.

The bonus was live music! A dozen gray-haired musicians were sitting in the front window of the funky, high-ceilinged old building, playing their hearts out. Fiddles, guitars, mandolin, dulcimer, bass, ukulele, piano. Scottish, Irish and Celtic tunes, one after another while we tapped our feet and ate our sandwiches.

I could feel my spirits rise as my shoes dried out. It was exactly what we needed, and the only people having more fun than the audience were the musicians.

When I was growing up, my mother made me take piano lessons, promising that such a skill was the key to popularity. After six years and no change in my social status, she let me quit. What she didn't tell me was that playing an instrument was a source of joy— for yourself and others. Forever.

Listening to those musicians at the Falling Rock Café, I felt envious of their delight and camaraderie. I wanted to belong the way they did, so alive and in tune, making something beautiful together. What a *joy!*

Visibility Unlimited

I'm in the boarding area, waiting for a flight to Phoenix. On an overhead computer screen I preview the weather at my destination city where visibility is described as "unlimited." I've never heard that said about Michigan.

It's late winter in my world where the visibility is particularly limited, not only by constant cloud cover but by snowbanks in my back yard as high as my head. I'm eager for something different, something warm and spacious.

From Phoenix, I take a shuttle to Prescott, up into the mountains where I am staying with a friend. She used to live in Michigan, too, but moved west because of the vistas, she tells me. Because on a clear day she can see forever and clear days are the norm.

One afternoon she takes me on a tour of the area and I exclaim about the gorgeous mountains. Finally, gently, she says, "We call these hills." And then she takes me to see a nearby lake where I can't resist observing that in Michigan we would call this a "pond."

Which is why, finally, I'm ready to trade mountains for lakes. Ready to return to the limited visibility of the place I call home.

LISTENING TO THE RAIN

While putting up the tent, I can't decide which is worse—the heat or the bugs. Sweat runs down the inside of my T-shirt as I grab the poles, attach the clips, enacting the familiar ritual with my husband.

Stopping to swat a mosquito, I drop my corner of the rain fly and glance at Dick who smiles patiently. Insects don't bother him; neither does heat.

"I think I'll put up the extra tarp," he says.

"But the sky is so blue," I say. He shrugs and goes about his work.

Two hours later, a rumble on the horizon turns into dark clouds and lightning flashes. Diving into the tent, Dick and I lie on sleeping bags and listen to rain on the tarp.

Overhead, thunder crashes louder than anything I've heard under a roof—crashes and grumbles and rumbles me away. Lying there amidst the noise and wind and fresh wet smells, I lose myself, float free like mist rising through pines.

And I wonder if death might be like this, a dissolving into the elements, knowing it was worth all the pain and doubt and difficulty.

Worth everything.

PEAK EXPERIENCE

We climbed steadily for four days and set up camp at 10,000 feet to rest before our descent. Deep valleys fell away into shadow while the white peaks of the Himalayas stood out along the horizon.

At a distance from our tents stood a tiny stone hut—a Buddhist place of worship—with a single prayer flag fluttering from a tall pole. I stepped through the low door and laid marigolds on the rough altar.

While most of our group of seven women wanted to relax, a few of us decided to hike to 13,000 feet the next day. Surely, we could see more if we stood higher!

Up the steep trail overhung with rhododendron, we passed a farm house where two men were building a roof with thin boards and pieces of slate. "It will take forever," I thought.

Three hours later we reached the summit and were enveloped in a cold white fog. We had climbed into a cloud. A slim boy stood before us with a dozen water buffalo. Our guide spoke with him and learned that he lived alone on the mountain with his herd. Fifteen years old. We gave him crackers and gum, and he let us take his picture.

"Not what we hoped for," one woman said. But I knew it was the unhoped-for, unexpected things that cranked open my mind, pierced my heart. During our return trip, I brooded about the solitary boy—his loneliness. Mine.

I picked my way carefully along the rocky path. Strange how it was always harder, going down. When we passed the farm house, the roof was finished.

BIGGER SELF

In a world of people wanting to slim down, my daughter and I are trying to plump up. Not physically but spiritually. We've figured out that the Ten Commandments and the Golden Rule and all the other guidelines for goodness can be summed up this way: Be Your Bigger Self.

You know your Bigger Self. It's the self you like best; the generous, loving, open-hearted person that you would like to be all the time. Instead, your Smaller Self often intervenes.

"I don't want to go to the anniversary party," I confess to Sara.

"Be big for an hour, Mom," she says. "Then you can come home and be small again."

You know your Smaller Self. It's the self you like least; the petty, critical, controlling person that you would like to never be but who is very hard to get rid of. In fact, the Smaller Self has an even tinier version. A friend with whom I have shared these conversations sometimes asks, "May I be my Micro-Self?"

I wish it weren't so hard to be my Bigger Self. Maybe I'm just hopeless; maybe I'm just human.

Either way, I'm going to the anniversary party—for an hour.

Two Wedding Rings

I wear two wedding rings—a fat gold band on my left hand and a slim silver one on my right. The silver ring has a pattern of double hearts and belonged to my Great Aunt Ruth, who was my grandmother's sister and the happiest member of our family.

Ruth didn't seem to judge anyone, including herself. I can still hear her robust laugh.

At age thirty-three she married a wealthy older man and their wedding date is engraved inside the ring I wear—June 24, 1919. They traveled to Alaska on their honeymoon, and I have a photograph of Ruth waving from a rope bridge above the Yukon River.

Ruth and Frederick had one child, a daughter who fell off her bike at age eight and suffered a concussion. "The nurse told us we could let her go to sleep," Ruth said, "but she never woke up." The following year Ruth and Frederick lost everything in the Depression.

After Frederick died from Parkinson's disease, Ruth lived alone. At age seventy-three, she remarried, traveled the world, and lived to celebrate her twentieth wedding anniversary. It was as if she believed in her own worth, her right to happiness, regardless.

When Ruth died, I was a young woman—too young to know much about suffering or seek her wisdom about how to face loss and embrace life. She left me only her example. And her ring.

ON THE RIVER

My husband holds the canoe steady as I climb in. Then he takes his place in the stern and we push off into the river. The paddle feels light and graceful in my hands as I dip, pull, lift, twist with ease. I can do this all day.

For the first hour, paddling seems effortless and I watch the scenery going by—the steep sandy bluffs topped with white pines, a tangle of cedar trees close to the water, leaning out.

By hour two, I feel some aching in my low back but when I cross my legs a different way, it disappears. I cross them another way and another.

When Dick suggests we stop for lunch, I am eager. We sit on a fallen log to eat our bread, cheese and apple slices—with a thermos of strong coffee. Climbing into the canoe again, I feel energetic for a while, ignore my sore back, my sore shoulders. Distract myself by looking for deer, for beaver.

My husband and I have been paddling together for over thirty years—and feel more tired and more grateful with each season. "Still here," we say as we shove off into the river.

Now, after four hours of paddling, I hurt all over and just hope I can make it to the landing without quitting. And I decide that I want to live out my life exactly this way. To keep going until I get there.

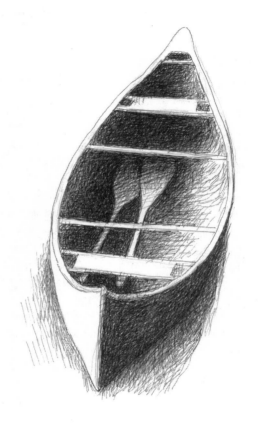

Studying Poetry

When my granddaughters were about eight and ten, I offered
to teach poetry as part of their homeschool curriculum. One
afternoon a week we sat around my dining room table to read and
write together.

It wasn't long before Emmy asked, "Why are we reading more boy
poets than girl poets?" A teachable moment. Because that's what
I studied in college, I explained. Literature written by white males
and taught by white males.

We spent the next year studying African-American and Native
American poetry. Followed by Chinese, Japanese, Latin American.
And lots of poetry by women.

For me, the best moments were when—after the discussion and
laughter—we sat in quiet concentration with only the soft squeak
of our pencils moving across the paper. Then we would read
our work aloud, with no disclaimers, no apologies. At the end of
each year, we memorized favorite poems and recited them to our
captive audience of parents and grandparents.

Poem by poem, our lives had grown larger, our bond stronger.
Edna St. Vincent Millay described this journey in her 1912 poem,
"Renascence", which brought her recognition at age nineteen, not
much older than my granddaughters.

> The world stands out on either side
> No wider than the heart is wide;
> Above the world is stretched the sky—
> No higher than the soul is high.
> (lines 203-206)

HOLY PLACES

It's almost too warm to jog but I lace up my shoes anyway. There's no traffic this morning because it's Sunday and the streets are quiet. The only cars are on their way to church or to the convenience store for coffee and a paper.

Down the block from my house is a small white church building that's used by various groups. A couple of guys are leaning against a pick-up truck having a cigarette before going inside. They nod as I go by.

Around the corner is the big Catholic church and the parking lot is full. A stained glass windows is tipped open and I can hear voices singing.

At the mile-mark, I pass the Lutheran church where people are getting out of their cars for the early service. Some of them smile and say, "Good morning." Some frown, as if to tell me that I should be in church.

"But I am in church!" I want to say. True, I'm wearing shorts and dripping with sweat, but I'm full of prayer, full of gratitude for my strong legs and these leafy trees and this holy place that is my neighborhood.

If God is anywhere, God is out here under the sky as well as under the roofs of the churches. And I'm out here, too, every Sunday—religiously.

Good News

I sit in my car waiting for the light to change, listening to the radio. The same old stories of war and politics. Suddenly, a big metal box flies out of the back of a pickup truck crossing the intersection—one of the busiest in the city.

At once, cars in four lanes stop while the driver of the pickup pulls over and runs to clean up the mess. Another guy parks his white van under the traffic light and gets out to help. Together, the men haul the box to the curb and pick up broken equipment.

Meanwhile, the light changes from green to red, green to red, again and again. But nobody honks, nobody moves, even the drivers who can't see what's going on. They understand it's a crisis and sit tight.

And somehow, I feel enormously cheered by what I'm seeing. I want to climb out of my car and thank someone, everyone! Here we all are, managing a difficult situation without anybody getting upset, without anybody telling us what to do. This is human beings at our best, I think. Self-regulating, capable, caring.

The bad news on my radio has turned to good news just beyond my windshield. Then traffic starts moving again and I turn left onto Division Street. Grateful beyond measure for this delay.

FRAGILE PEOPLE

When my daughter was twenty-four years old, she was diagnosed with cancer and given a grim prognosis. Sara was student teaching at the time and had just become engaged. Suddenly everything was on hold—for her, and the people who loved her.

In the early weeks of the crisis, we all grappled with our shock and terror, determined to come down on the side of hope. Her fiancé never missed a beat and insisted they keep planning the wedding. And I did what moms do: made chicken soup and washed dishes at her apartment.

I rearranged my work schedule to be with Sara as much as possible. One morning, I was called out of a meeting to take her phone call. "I don't know," she said, "I was just swept with fear."

Of course she was. So was I. All day long I lurched from despair to faith and back again, forgetting to eat, to breathe.

But slowly, slowly Sara got well, and seven months later she got married. Long afterward, I asked what helped her survive those terrible months, and she listed the people who were close to her.

"Your voice," she said. "Hearing your voice."

And I thought about the miracle of fragile people helping fragile people. I think about it still.

FLAG

When I moved to Traverse City from Chicago in 1970, I went to work at the Record-Eagle, back when the newspaper was owned by the Batdorff family. I'd been there only a few days when I noticed that the American flag flying above the building was in tatters and I walked into Bob Batdorff's office to tell him.

He was the publisher of the paper and later that day he walked down Front Street himself and bought a new flag.

In Chicago I had worked for a multi-national company and never met the president whose office, in any event, was on the West Coast. I liked the idea that in Traverse City my voice might be heard. A lot has changed since 1970, but I want to believe that I—or any citizen—can still make a difference.

I'm always moved when I attend a City Commission meeting to see others like myself, ordinary people in jeans and sneakers, who overcome their fear and step up to the microphone.

Because when I say "Not my back yard," I'm not just talking about the few square feet behind my house. I'm talking about the whole city, about which I feel a very personal sense of ownership. So whenever I get discouraged I remember Bob Batdorff and the new flag.

EIGHT CRAYONS

There was a time when all I needed to be happy was a box of eight Crayola crayons and a coloring book. Stretched out on the living room floor, I would color for hours in a state of bliss.

Then, I noticed that Crayola sold a box of sixteen crayons. It was great having twice as many colors but it didn't make me twice as happy. Finally, the store started selling an enormous box with a flip-top lid that seemed to contain hundreds of crayons, and I received one.

What I discovered was that the colors weren't that different from each other, so having dozens to choose from was meaningless. Worse, it distracted me from doing what I loved.

That was long ago and now the whole world has exploded with choices, making it harder and harder to assemble the ingredients of happiness. Something is always missing. But I've learned that even with a flip-top box, more is just more—not better. With eight crayons, I could mix all the other colors and be creative.

Coloring with a seven-year-old recently, I felt a surge of forgotten bliss. "Here's a marker with glitter," she said.

"Thanks," I said. "I'm happy with this blue crayon."

MINDLESS TASKS

In the middle of an essay, I hear the buzzer that signals my clothes are dry. Gratefully, I leave the task of writing to take up the task of folding laundry.

Folding laundry requires minimal skills and causes no stress. Thank goodness for mindless tasks, I think. They buffer me against the other tasks, like writing, which requires maximal skills, skills that sometimes seem to vanish in the middle of a paragraph.

Not only are mindless tasks a welcome interruption, they actually seem to enhance my performance when I return to mindful ones. Walking to the basement to collect my laundry, I collect my thoughts as well.

It was a mysterious thing, how I could sit in front of my computer searching for the right word and not find it until I sorted socks. It certainly wasn't the message my parents gave me. Nobody ever said, "If at first you don't succeed, go fold laundry."

I had to discover it for myself, this necessary rhythm of mindful and mindless activity. By the time the shirts are folded, my mind has unfolded. The words are tumbling out like clean clothes from the dryer right into my basket. Warm and fresh and ready to wear.

Voices in the Dark

When I was a child, I didn't need a nightlight. What comforted me was the sound of my parents' voices downstairs in the living room. Lying in the dark, I would hold very still and listen. Not for their words exactly, just the soft murmur of conversation.

If I didn't hear them, I would get out of bed and tiptoe to the door. There, I strained to detect the slightest sound—even the rustle of a newspaper—to confirm their presence.

If everything was silent, I would go to the top of the stairs and call down, "Mom?"

Her musical voice would reply, "Yes?"

Then I would simply say, "Good night." And two voices would say, "Good night." It was enough to send me back to sleep.

While there was much that my parents did not give me, *could* not give me—of love and wisdom and emotional honesty—they gave me what they had. It's all any of us can give and we look for ways to forgive the rest, be forgiven. My parents gave me what they had—and they were there every evening in the living room, talking quietly together.

"Yes?" my mother would say but it wasn't a question. It was the answer.

ACKNOWLEDGEMENTS

Writing these acknowledgements has proved harder than writing any essay. Words fail in the presence of so much gratitude, but they're what I have. First, I want to thank the listeners of Interlochen Public Radio who have commented on my essays over the years, shared their stories, and asked if I have a collection. Until now, I've had to say no.

This all began when Peter Payette, Executive Director of IPR, called me in 2003 while I was writing for the Traverse City Record-Eagle. "I think your columns could be adapted for radio," he said. Yes, they could. The IPR team has been enormously helpful in editing, producing, previewing, and posting essays on the website: David Cassleman, Deb Poltorak, Aaron Selbig, Morgan Springer and former reporter, Linda Stephan.

Publishing a collection became a reality when I found Arbutus Press and Susan Bays who believed in the project and introduced me to the realities of getting a book put together. Susan's experience, hard work, and humor have made it happen. Credit is due to copy editor Emmy Holman who persuaded me to curb my enthusiasm for dashes—almost. She also caught countless other errors, saving me from myself.

Poet and teacher Holly Wren Spaulding has been a trusted mentor, not only for her editing skills but for her belief that good writing can change the world. In one of her workshops, she said, "There's room for all of us," which has helped me more than I can say.

Artist Joyce Koskenmaki has been an remarkable partner in this endeavor, contributing her stunning illustrations which have adding so much meaning and beauty. She has helped me see with new eyes and we have become friends along the way. A gift.

Thank you to good friend Michael DeAgro of Zenki Lotus Institute who pushed me out of my comfort zone to publish a collection. To Amy Reynolds of Horizon Books who offered encouragement. To Matt May of Inacomp Computer who provided technical support. To Amy Barritt and Peg Siciliano of the History Center who retrieved photos.

I salute the community of writers and artists in this region who support the arts and each other, including the National Writers Series and Michigan Writers. I am especially thankful to my TSO poetry group for lessons in excellence and to my prose writing group, the Inkhearts, who believed I could do this and helped.

Special gratitude to those friends whose wisdom and kindness have nourished me and whose stories I have told. Also to family members, Bob and Candy Anderson, Derek Boven, Marilyn Wildes, Susan and David Parks, Stephanie Parks, Emilia Butryn, who allowed me to write about the experiences we've shared. Bless you.

And to the three without-whom people in my life: husband, Richard Parks; daughter, Sara Boven; sister (in-law), Kay Koop. You make everything possible.

About the Artist

JOYCE KOSKENMAKI

Joyce Koskenmaki's illustrations and paintings have been shown nationally and internationally. She has received many grants and awards and has taught at six different colleges and universities. She now lives in the Upper Peninsula of Michigan, near the forests of her childhood.

She walks in the woods every day, surrounded by the trees which are a constant presence in her work, both as subject and metaphor: she sees them as companions and protectors.

Also illustrated by Joyce Koskenmaki:

Naked in the Stream: Isle Royale Stories
Hidden in the Trees: An Isle Royale Sojourn

About the Author

Karen Anderson is a writer who lives and works in Traverse City, Michigan.

She wrote a weekly column in the *Traverse City Record-Eagle* for 30 years. Since 2005, she has contributed a weekly essay to Interlochen Public Radio which is also archived on the IPR website. She has published several poems in the *Dunes Review*.

Karen has a master's degree in English Literature from the University of Michigan and is retired from Northwestern Michigan College where she was director of marketing and public relations. She enjoys camping, canoeing, reading, writing, listening, learning.